THE SECRET LIFE OF INSECTS

'These stories are fully cognizant of Horror's past, but they also provide clear signposts for Horror's possible future. Very deft, smart stories that manage to do in ten pages what most novels struggle to accomplish in thirty times that. Esquinca is a writer to watch.'

— Brian Evenson, award-winning author of
Song for the Unraveling of the World

'From short, punchy, *Twilight Zone*-ish stories to longer, far more insidious dances with horror and madness, Esquinca weaves reality with illusion deftly in *The Secret Life of Insects*, an excellent collection. Recommended!'

— Elizabeth Engstrom, author of
When Darkness Loves Us and *Black Ambrosia*

'Bernardo Esquinca's haunting, original stories spin out implications like spider silk: light, strong . . . and very dangerous.'

— Michael Cisco, author of *The Divinity Student*

'Bernardo Esquinca is a writer who knows that fear is another form of desire. Of the desire for the dark, the desire for the mysterious, and the desire for life in death. His writing grabs you and takes you by the hand through obsessions where what is beautiful and monstrous in humanity dwells. Read him: you're going to be terrified and amazed at the same time.'

— Mónica Ojeda, author of *Jawbone*

'Bernardo Esquinca traces the veil between the natural and supernatural, and with a doctor's precision, he slits that perimeter in order to reach through and drag back something completely outside the realm of our own comprehension. The fourteen tales within this breathtaking collection don't come from our world, but beyond it. *The Secret Life of Insects* firmly establishes Esquinca as a rising dark star of horror.'

— Clay McLeod Chapman, author of *Ghost Eaters*

ABOUT THE AUTHOR

BERNARDO ESQUINCA's fiction is characterized by a fusion of the genres of the supernatural and the crime novel. Born in Guadalajara in 1972, he is the author of several novels and story collections, including one translated into English, *The Owls Are Not What They Seem* (2018). His short story 'Señor Ligotti' was nominated for the prestigious Shirley Jackson Award in 2021, and his novel *Toda la sangre* was made into a television series by the production company Lionsgate+. He lives in Mexico City, surrounded by ancient gods, urban legends, and naughty ghosts.

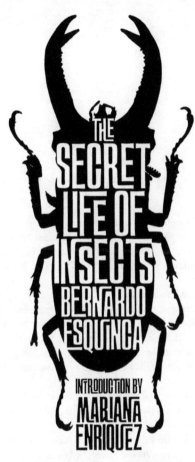

THE SECRET LIFE OF INSECTS

BERNARDO ESQUINCA

INTRODUCTION BY
MARIANA ENRIQUEZ

TRANSLATED BY
JAMES D. JENKINS

ILLUSTRATED BY
LUIS PEREZ OCHANDO

VALANCOURT BOOKS
Richmond, Virginia
MMXXIII

Published by Valancourt Books, Richmond, Virginia
http://www.valancourtbooks.com

ISBN 978-1-954321-95-3 (trade hardcover)
ISBN 978-1-954321-96-0 (trade paperback)
Also available as an electronic book.

Cover by Vince Haig
Set in Bembo Book MT

Contents

'The Secret Life of Insects' originally published as 'La vida secreta de los insectos' in *Los niños de paja* (Editorial Almadía, 2008).

'The Wizard's Hour' originally published as 'La hora del mago' in *El libro de los dioses* (Editorial Almadía, 2020).

'Where I'm Going, It's Always Night' originally published as 'Adonde voy siempre es de noche' in *Demonia* (Editorial Almadía, 2011).

'The Dream of the Fisherman's Wife' originally published as 'El sueño de la esposa del pescador' in *El libro de los dioses* (Editorial Almadía, 2020).

'The Paradoxical Man' originally published as 'El hombre de la paradoja' in *El libro de los dioses* (Editorial Almadía, 2020).

'Leprosy in the Walls' originally published as 'La lepra de las paredes' in *Letras Libres* (Dec. 2019).

'Señor Ligotti' originally published as 'El señor Ligotti' in *El libro de los dioses* (Editorial Almadía, 2020).

'Come to Me' originally published as 'Ven a mí' in *Mar Negro* (Editorial Almadía, 2014).

'Demoness' originally published as 'Demonia' in *Demonia* (Editorial Almadía, 2011).

'Dream of Me' originally published as 'Sueña conmigo' in *Mar Negro* (Editorial Almadía, 2014).

'Pan's Noontide' originally published as 'La hora meridiana de Pan' in *El libro de los dioses* (Editorial Almadía, 2020).

'Tlatelolco Confidential' originally published as 'La otra noche de Tlatelolco' in *Mar Negro* (Editorial Almadía, 2014).

'Sea of Tranquility, Ocean of Storms' originally published as 'Mar de la Tranquilidad, Océano de las Tormentas' in *Mar Negro* (Editorial Almadía, 2014).

'Manuscript Found in an Empty Apartment' originally published as 'Manuscrito encontrado en un departamento vacío' in *Demonia* (Editorial Almadía, 2011).

Foreword

by Mariana Enríquez

Sometimes Bernardo Esquinca's obsessions lie hidden in his direct and powerful stories, but most often they're right there in the open: brooding ideas that buzz in the night before slumbering in the corners of sleep. Magical thinking, insane asylums, secondhand bookstores and their peculiar treasures, ancient gods, lovers' breakups, ruins. The influence of his guiding lights seeps between the lines of his stories as well: Amparo Dávila, Thomas Ligotti, E. A. Poe, Lovecraft. Esquinca is a very smart writer and well aware of his tradition; he has taken an area and haunted it: Mexico City, and especially its historic center, whose intensity, inequality, and mixture of cultures serve as his tapestry and background, landscape and essence. Occasionally he goes further afield, spreading dread through other provinces, like Guanajuato, or even other countries, but not often. Calle Donceles, the ruins of the Templo Mayor, the Colonia Doctores and Roma neighborhoods: you start to look at them differently after reading these stories, because Esquinca scatters his broken, insomniac characters in these familiar places.

Another thing about Bernardo Esquinca's stories is their decisive opening lines, surely a nod to his other passion: true crime. It's all there, at the beginning. He grabs like a furious tentacle: 'Two items of interest: (1) Today I'm going to talk to my wife for the first time in two years. (2) My wife is dead. She passed away two years ago under strange circumstances.' Thus begins 'The Secret Life of Insects', a short and powerful tale featuring a forensic entomologist, a classic Esquinca detective character, somewhere between investigatorial and ghoulish.

The 'other' literature

Popular culture has many forms of expression, some looked down upon: the horror story, though fortunately less and less so, is still one of them. It's what Esquinca calls 'the other literature'. Interesting tidbits, anecdotes, popular science magazines, conspiracy theories, ufology, the compilation of mythical information crossed with superstition. Bernardo Esquinca uses those voices that surround us and takes them seriously. The influence of Poe is clear, but also that of those voices that enter madness not through the door of the great lords, but through the commoners' entrance.

The protagonists of Esquinca's stories are often books, not princely tomes or mysterious occult treatises, but the ones you can buy from any street vendor for a peso. The implication is even more disturbing: it's not volumes bound in human skin or illuminated medieval manuscripts that contain revelations and open portals – not *The King in Yellow* or the *Necronomicon* – but those ordinary paperbacks with silly illustrations whose throwaway theories we scoff at.

The protagonist of 'Manuscript Found in an Empty Apartment' finds clues about his brother's death in a book that leads him to Guanajuato: 'It had been a long time since I'd been to that city, and as I passed through the tunnels underneath it I remembered that it was mysterious by nature; that despite its touristy side, it gave the impression of containing a secret.' Architecture, old books, passageways, neighbors: Esquinca's mad, mystical, everyday horror, the poisonous urban landscape, the towers and buildings like new fortresses, far from the castles now, but very close to the slums.

The ruins of the returning past

Romantic relationships in Esquinca's stories are sometimes as threatening as ruins; what's left of them is mysterious and trembles. 'Come to Me' feeds off everyday trash: in this case, the flyers for love potions and other magical operations we see in the streets stuck to lampposts, and to which we seemingly pay no attention. But no doubt there are many people who use them. Maybe even we ourselves – myself – have a secret to hide: visits to the witch who receives clients over a plastic tablecloth in a room smelling of fried food and jasmine. The story is almost a rewrite of W.W. Jacobs's 'The Monkey's Paw', but is unbelievably more macabre; it might be the most horrifying story collected here. Desire and despair as triggers of horror: love as a circle of hell. 'Distress and blind faith in a magical solution,' says Laurinda, the protagonist, a woman living in an almost unimaginable nightmare.

The past, ruins, and love form a dangerous triangle in the most political story here, 'Tlatelolco Confidential': 'That day marked their six-month anniversary; they decided to celebrate by attending the rally at Plaza de las Tres Culturas to hand out flyers in support of the students' movement. And in a single second the world disintegrated in a hail of bullets.' I won't say what happens, but I will add another quote, which tells how that piece of land, that square, demands blood. And gets it. 'Tlatelolco was the final stronghold of the Aztecs during the Spanish conquest, and it makes perfect sense for their return to begin from this epicenter. Every tomb excavated, every fragment of pyramid that comes to light, only confirms that they never left, they've just been waiting for the right moment to take back what's theirs. And for that an enormous sacrifice was needed.'

What ground are we walking over, what is it we're stepping on, what secrets lie hidden beneath the surface, not only of the streets we stroll down so calmly, but under our skin, behind our eyes?

The sick and the mad

The great writer on madness was E. A. Poe, of whom Esquinca is an avowed fan, and about whom he has written quite a lot. Like Poe, he is interested in insanity. 'Sea of Tranquility, Ocean of Storms' is about hereditary madness and has one of those terrific and irresistible opening lines: 'In my family there were always secrets, but madness cannot be hidden.' Cousin Rodolfo's delusions and conspiracy theories are dangerously similar to paranoid theories on internet forums (in fact, Rodolfo spends a lot of time there). And then there's 'Dream of Me', one of my favorites, about a collector of haunted dolls who mixes his own chilling story with the horrible – and wonderful – biographies of the dolls in his collection, somewhere between Freudian uncanny and urban legend.

There is cosmic horror in Esquinca, in the aforementioned 'Sea of Tranquility', for example, but there is also a lot of religious horror: he acknowledges his Jesuit education. Like in the key novella 'Demoness', where taking as his point of departure a personal experience, which the author does not fully reveal, he confronts science and faith in the mode of *The Exorcist* with an expository coldness, almost a commentary, that combines sex, teenage masturbatory acts, anthropology, rituals, theater, ecstasy, a class reunion, and demonology in a stripped-down setting.

Each little revelation, moreover, is almost a trigger for another possible story. Bernardo Esquinca's tales are usually short, but they contain such a large amount of information that each paragraph could grow into its own branch, until they formed a whole grove of true and false legends, a black forest of horror.

The master of the tale

You can tell that Bernardo Esquinca can't help himself when

it comes to inserting theories about the short story, the horror genre, the whys and wherefores of writing, into his tales. Here are some I've found in his work as a whole:

1) 'I've never really understood where a story comes from, if it's born or if it's really in some parallel dimension, just waiting for a writer to reach into the darkness and pull a dead rabbit from it.'

2) 'Usually the best stories are just around the corner; sometimes all you have to do is open a magazine, and if it's a tabloid, all the better.'

3) 'I think fear is an altered state that the brain comes to need, like a drug. That's why the horror writers I most admire are never short of readers.'

4) 'Don't knock liars: they're great storytellers. In any case, what you believe says a lot more about you than it does about me. That's the key to every story.'

5) 'I suppose the best stories are like abandoned houses that nobody wants to stay in, but which you can't stop thinking about after spending a night in them.'

I could go on, but I'd rather the reader look for themselves and find this decalogue hidden in these stories that are the work of an elegant hand and a somewhat twisted mind.

★

I know Bernardo, I've met him several times in real life and on Zoom and at lectures and at the house of our mutual friend Jorge Alderete in Mexico City and at the Oaxaca festival, and we trade emails and messages. He introduced me to Amparo Dávila; we share a passion for Ligotti, Mónica Ojeda, and Liliana Blum's *El monstruo pentápodo*. But I want to tell you two little non-literary anecdotes that, for me, are unforgettable.

When I was in Mexico City, I wanted to visit the cemetery (or *panteón*, as they call it in Mexico, a term that seems very odd to an Argentinian like me) of San Fernando, in the historic center. It's one of the oldest and has various legends associated with it, in addition to splendid tombs. He knows about my funerary passion and wanted to show me this gloomy beauty. Unfortunately the Panteón was closed: a sign said it was for reasons of safety, due to the devastating earthquake of 2017, whose epicenter was Puebla but which also affected Mexico City. Bernardo, with his good manners and gentle voice – he's a delightful person, like almost all horror writers – started yelling for the caretaker to see if he could make an exception for us. Next to the Panteón there was a mutilated dog, possibly run over by a car, its guts hanging out. A few yards away some grim-faced boys were smoking. I tried to hide my fear, and I think I did a good job, but I was scared. I didn't want to see the ghostly caretaker appear, if he existed. I didn't want to hear the door of one of the burial niches fall open.

A little while later, Bernardo sent me a message with a photo: it was an altar that had appeared near his house in Colonia Doctores. I can't tell you what that figure on it was, only that it provoked an authentic superstitious repulsion, an evil and malignant veneration, with details I prefer not to remember. Yet I think, as I write this foreword, that I should describe the image better, because it deserves it. I know I downloaded it from my phone to my computer. But it's not there now. I can't find it. It's not in the recent images, or with the unorganized ones, or in the folders where I keep pictures that inspire or terrify me – which is usually the same thing. I didn't save the message, and I don't know why: I usually delete when I have too many unimportant messages, but I wouldn't have deleted the photo of that thing. I check my inbox, in case my memory is playing tricks on me and the altar to that urban god was sent there instead. Not there either. It's vanished. I don't know if I should ask him to resend it, I don't dare, and I don't know if it still exists, if it'll be waiting for me when I visit him, and the figure on the altar and I will look into each other's eyes at last.

There are true things in this world noticed only by a single pair of eyes.

Carmen María Machado

The Secret Life of Insects

Two items of interest: (1) Today I'm going to talk to my wife for the first time in two years. (2) My wife is dead. She passed away two years ago under strange circumstances.

It's my day off and our 'date' isn't until tonight, so I'll take advantage of my free time to go to the beach. Lucia loved the sea. She wouldn't swim in it; she had too much respect for it. But she would go for long walks along the shore and loved letting the waves lick her bare feet. Oddly enough, she told me once that when she died, the last place she would want her ashes scattered was the sea. 'One night I dreamt I was dying, and all I could do was swim and swim through the darkness at the bottom of the ocean, like a blind fish.' I didn't pay much attention at the time – nobody takes it seriously when a healthy person talks about their death – but it comes to mind now as I put some cans of beer in the cooler and grab a book to lie down and read in the sun.

I'm a forensic entomologist. My job is to study the insects that overrun cadavers and leave clues behind to help catch killers. The bugs like to lay their eggs on the victim's face, or in their eyes or nose. The trick is to connect the life cycles of the insects with the stages of the body's decomposition, which allows you to approximate the time of death. In other words, it's like a kind of clock. You can even determine whether the body has been moved from another spot. Insects also like to feed on rotting flesh. Among them flies, beetles, spiders, ants, wasps, and centipedes. And they're voracious:

the remains of an adult human left exposed in the open air can be devoured rapidly. Entomologists call this necrophile fauna the 'squadrons of death'.

My most famous case to date was this: A family moves into a house. Two months later they find the corpse of a murdered child in the basement and report it to the authorities. The police zero in on them as the prime suspects. However, by analyzing the insects that had colonized the body I was able to determine that the crime had been committed before the people in question moved into that residence. So the blame fell on the former tenants – an elderly couple who turned out to be the boy's grandparents – the true perpetrators. A whole family had their skin saved by a handful of mites.

Six months ago, my friend Leonardo told me he knew a medium. He assured me she wasn't a fraud and could help me communicate with my wife. I heard him out politely but declined: I belong to the world of science, the rational world. What's more, I've seen too many atrocities and mutilated corpses to believe there's a God, much less an afterlife. Evil is rampant everywhere, and there's nothing capable of stopping it. It's better if there isn't a life after death, since most likely evil would continue its reign there. He insisted: 'You've got nothing to lose by trying. And if it works, you'll get the answers to what's been tormenting you. I'll pay for the session.' He failed to convince me. It wasn't until three months ago, when I decided to take Lucia's case into my own hands, that I began seriously considering the possibility.

The smell of the gases given off by a corpse is what attracts the first insects. They can detect it well before the human nose can. Sometimes they even swarm a person during his death throes. The eggs laid by certain insects have a short embryonic period and all hatch at the same time, resulting in a mass of larvae moving like an alien entity over the body. The larvae are white and burrow immediately into the subcutaneous tissue. With the help of certain bacteria and enzymes they liquefy it and feed by means of a continuous suction. As time passes and if the corpse isn't found – after six months, let's say – other bugs come along that leave it completely dry. Everything is used: hair, skin, nails. Sometimes the forensic examiners find nothing but bones.

I said before that my wife died under strange circumstances. Her body turned up in a forest an hour away from this port city. The night before, I had dropped her off at the airport; she was headed to visit her mother in Mexico City. In the dead of night, when I was asleep, Lucia came back home, saying her flight had been canceled because of the weather and that she'd return to the airport later and catch another plane. I heard her between dreams. She got into bed and laid her head on my chest, as was her habit. When I awoke, she was gone; I assumed she hadn't wanted to disturb me and had taken a taxi. A few hours later, when I was told of the grisly discovery, I decided I wouldn't be the one who handled the case. My boss understood and sent Alejandro, one of his students at the Faculty of Medicine, to collect the body. I didn't want to know a single one of the details. Lucia was dead. She'd been murdered. That was enough for me.

No one knows for sure where insects come from. Some scholars claim that they originated from myriapods, many-legged animals with respiratory tracts. Others speculate they evolved from crustaceans. What is certain is that in the Devonic period, 400 million years ago, earthbound insects already existed in the hottest and wettest swampy regions. And in the Mississippian period, 350 million years ago, they underwent their first evolutionary explosion with the appearance of wings and the ability to fly. The most persistent and evolved of them all is, of course, the cockroach. Interestingly, I've never seen a cockroach around a corpse.

Since my wife's killer hasn't been found, I decided to review the case. I analyzed the samples collected by Alejandro and found several serious errors. Among them, one that left me puzzled: a mistake in calculating the time of death. Lucia was found in the woods by a group of campers at nine a.m. Alejandro determined she had been dead an hour by then. My analysis indicated that she had been dead at least six hours. That is, she had died in the middle of the night, when she was supposed to be asleep in my arms. And since I didn't know exactly what time Lucia had left the house that night, everything got quite confusing. Leonardo had a theory: she was already dead when she 'visited' me in bed. 'It's something the dead often do,' he told me. 'They come to say goodbye to those they loved.' Unhinged by the whole business, I finally gave in to the idea of the medium. We had an appointment two days ago. I brought her some of Lucia's things she had asked for: clothes, objects, photos. Then she gave me an exact date and time. Tonight at nine o'clock. 'She'll call you on the telephone,' she said in a solemn tone.

I have a recurring dream about Lucia. First I see the insects clandestinely devouring her body. I arrive at the crime scene and realize she's still alive, and I try to get them off her, but it's impossible: there are too many of them. She cries out to me: 'You brought them to me.' Then she can't talk anymore because they start coming out of her mouth. That's when I close her eyes and I wake up.

Only a few seconds until nine p.m. I haven't eaten anything all day; I'm not hungry. I'm lying in bed. The phone is on the nightstand. I look at the ceiling and notice that it's cracked and peeling: it needs a good coat of paint. I spot a cobweb in a corner. Some dead insects are trapped in it. Suddenly, one of them trembles: it's alive and struggling to free itself.

Just then the phone rings.

One . . .

Two . . .

Three . . .

Four . . .

Five times . . .

I pick up.

I hear the sound of the sea.

The Wizard's Hour

At first, Dragan didn't connect what was happening with the baby chair. His wife had bought it at a discount store and for a month now they'd been putting little Lena in it with very good results. It had several buttons to adjust its rhythmic motions, as well as a hidden speaker from which a constantly changing stream of noises emerged. Lena would fall into a long, deep sleep, and Dragan was able to work in his study without interruptions.

The first few days, the sounds the chair made caught their attention, and they even gave them names. There was one that was muffled and monotonous, like the sound of waves breaking on the shore, which reminded Dragan and his wife of their desire to get out of the city, so they called it 'Vacation'; another was melodious and resembled the background music at a workplace, so they referred to it as 'Office'; and yet another, vaguely hypnotic, that made Dragan think of an act he'd seen at a circus when he was a kid, which he named 'The Wizard's Hour'. Soon all these sound effects stopped being new and just became another part of the landscape of their home; a background noise for their thoughts and conversations.

Everything was going fine until Dragan started experiencing the Episodes. He was just putting Lena in the chair when suddenly he found himself in the hardware section at a department store, holding a drill. He didn't remember how he'd gotten there, nor why he was standing there holding a tool he didn't need. He returned home, more thoughtful than frightened, telling himself he needed to work less and sleep more.

When he got home, he wasn't sure whether he should tell his wife about the incident. She greeted him with a question that puzzled him:

'How did it go at the store?'

Stunned, he only managed to respond:

'Fine.'

To make things even weirder, she said:

'Why didn't you buy anything? Were the drills too expensive?'

Dragan improvised a response, deciding not to say anything about his sense of lost time. Like many people who find themselves caught up in a strange and inexplicable event, he acted like nothing had happened and trusted that it wouldn't happen again.

But he was wrong. Two days later he experienced another Episode. After putting Lena in the seat, he looked up and found himself on the roof of a building. He was standing at the safety rail, looking out on the city skyline as a strong wind lashed his face. He felt panic. Under normal circumstances, Dragan never went up on a roof because he suffered from vertigo. But there he was, on top of an unknown building, as if some force had carried him there against his will. It took him several minutes to collect himself, to recover the ability to move safely and be able to leave the building.

That night he didn't sleep. At what point had his mind crossed some unknown border? Should he consult a specialist? And, above all, should he worry his wife by letting her see how fragile his psyche was? With little Lena at stake, wouldn't she rush out of the house, taking their daughter and everything else? He decided to try the anti-anxiety pills in the medicine cabinet. It all came down to stress: fatherhood, the backlog of work, bills to pay. He took a pill and managed to sleep for a few hours.

But things got worse. In the next Episode, Dragan found himself standing at a cash register as an employee handed him money. He was dumbfounded until the woman told him:

'Your change, sir.'

He took the money and looked at the shopping bag he was holding. Inside was a pistol. He was on the verge of saying something, but the people in line behind him looked impatient, so he turned around and left the place. Fortunately his wife wasn't home; he could hide the gun, and the bullets he'd bought, in the closet. He put them in a shoebox, which he then placed in the back of the closet.

Pale, sweating, Dragan went to the bathroom and splashed water on his face. Then he looked in the mirror, and what he saw was the reflection of a frightened, confused man who had ceased to have control over his actions. This had to stop. He would take action, he would regain his willpower. It was then that he heard the noise in the background. That sound from his childhood, to which he had stopped paying attention, and which now returned to his ears with the force of a revelation. *The Wizard's Hour*. How had he not realized it before? He couldn't explain it, but he was convinced that ridiculous music was causing the Episodes. He left the bathroom and in the living room met his wife, who had just put Lena in the baby seat. He greeted her with a grimace and, pretending he had work to do, locked himself in his study.

That night, when his wife and daughter were sleeping, he went to the living room and checked Lena's baby seat. He was looking for something that would show who manufactured it. On the lower part of the chair back he found a label sewn to the cloth. He read: *Ligotti Industries*. And a phone number.

Not caring what time it was, Dragan went to the phone and dialed. He had a feeling that somebody would answer.

The voice on the other end was indistinct. It could have been an old man's, but also a child's.

'Come and see me. I'm waiting for you.'

2

Dragan brought the pistol along.

He drove down side streets in search of the address the voice on the phone had given him. It was in an area with offices and shops. He had no trouble finding the place: it was the only building lit up at that hour of night. The door was open. He climbed a winding staircase to the second floor. At the end of the carpeted hallway he saw a rectangle of light. He walked with unsteady steps as he felt for the pistol in his pants pocket.

He went through the doorway and came upon rows of boxes stacked from floor to ceiling. Hundreds of boxes. Each contained a baby seat identical to Lena's. In one corner there was a desk. The man sitting behind it motioned for Dragan to come closer. His age, like his voice, was hard to make out. Tall and thin, he was wearing a tuxedo, with a bowler hat and a black cape. Dragan felt a chill.

It was the circus wizard from his childhood.

'Congratulations,' he said. 'Not everyone solves the puzzle and makes it here.'

Dragan just stood there, incredulous.

'What did you do to me?' he asked.

The man in the cape and hat made a bow over the desk and raised an eyebrow.

'What I did to EVERYONE,' he answered. 'Don't get any ideas about being special.'

He gave a wave of his hand, encompassing the boxes.

'I sent out thousands of orders. And thousands more are on the way.'

Dragan rubbed his eyes, as if trying to wake up from a nightmare.

'I know you. When I was a kid I saw you at the circus,' and then, almost pleading, he added, 'Don't tell me it's not personal.'

The man in the cape and hat leaned back in the chair and put his hands on his stomach, which was suddenly swollen.

'I'm sorry to disappoint you. What you see is only a representation picked by your mind to give me a shape. I'm not responsible for it. What I *have* done is get into your head.'

Dragan pulled out the pistol and pointed it at him.

'Whatever you did, fix it. Or I'll kill you.'

The man in the cape and hat burst into a strange fit of laughter. Something that was like a croak at first, and then the babbling of a baby. Dragan trembled and made an effort to hold his hand steady.

'You think I won't shoot?' he asked, cocking the gun.

The man in the cape and hat opened his eyes wide and nodded. His eyes bulged, as if there was something behind the sockets that was much larger than the body containing it.

'Oh yes,' he said. 'Of course you'll shoot.'

Dragan felt his hand moving.

'What's your serial number?' the man in the cape and hat asked, rifling through some papers on the desk. 'Here it is: 346,975. Indeed, you're programmed to shoot.'

He paused and then looked up.

'Only not at me.'

Dragan stifled a scream. No matter how hard he fought, the barrel of the gun remained pointed at his own temple.

'Please, no,' he begged, sobbing.

The man in the cape and hat smiled. It was a toothless smile, like that of an old man. Or a newborn.

Click.

The trigger hit the firing pen, but there was no bang. Dragan took a deep breath, relieved: the pistol was unloaded.

'Now go,' the man in the cape and hat said. 'Go back home to your wife and daughter.'

Dragan wiped his tears with the back of his hand.

'Why are you toying with me?' he asked in a faint voice.

The man in the cape and hat looked impatient. The appointment was at an end.

'Because I *can*.'

Dragan turned around and walked towards the door. As he crossed the threshold, the man spoke to him once more.

'Wait.'

Dragan stopped but didn't turn around. He was sure that if he did, this time he would see the real form behind that indistinct voice. And what he saw would be engraved on his pupils so that even little Lena would be able to see it.

'What?'

'Keep that pistol oiled,' said the voice.

Before letting him leave, it added:

'One of these days I'm going to ask you to use it.'

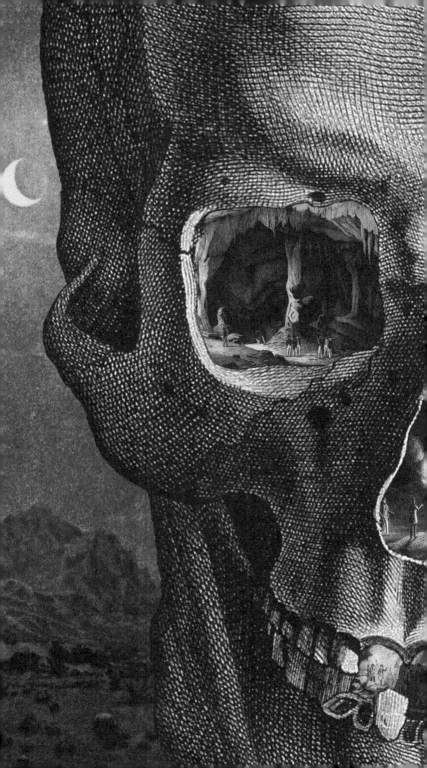

Where I'm Going It's Always Night

The man walked along the side of the road with his backpack on his shoulder. Two cars drove past, but he didn't even glance at them. Everardo thought it was odd he didn't ask for a lift: there was nothing around for miles but trees. He felt curious. He slowed down until the van pulled up alongside him and lowered the passenger side window.

'Where are you headed?'

The man had a thick beard and wore a cap with earflaps. He seemed to be lost deep in thought. He looked at Everardo with intense blue eyes and replied:

'To the mountains.'

Everardo stopped the vehicle and unlocked the door.

'I'll take you. If you keep going at that pace, it'll be the middle of the night by the time you get there.'

The man got in and put his backpack on the back seat.

'Where I'm going it's always night,' he said in a raspy voice. 'My name's Jacobo.'

They shook hands. Everardo put his foot on the gas again.

'What do you do?'

'I'm a spelunker. I spend a lot of my time in underground caves.'

'But why all alone? Aren't you supposed to do it in groups?'

Jacobo's eyes were fixed on the landscape outside the window: pine trees, yellow hills, the overcast afternoon sky.

'I prefer going alone. I'm a bounty hunter.'

'Damn, that sounds like something out of an old Western . . . Don't tell me you look for gold mines.'

'Nothing like that.' Jacobo ran his hand through his beard. 'One day I read in the paper that a lady was offering a reward for the body of her son, a young cave explorer who'd died in an accident a month before. The boy had fallen a long way down and the rescuers couldn't reach his body. Not to brag, but I set the national record for descents. Thanks to me, the lady was able to bury her son . . . Afterwards I started doing it for a living: now I travel around to different regions retrieving the bodies of my less fortunate colleagues.'

Everardo lit a cigarette. After a bend in the road, the mountains appeared on the horizon. He looked at the sky's weak glow: it wouldn't be long till nightfall.

'And now you're going to . . . work?'

'Exactly.'

'What happened?' Everardo asked, not hiding his growing morbid interest.

Jacobo fixed his blue eyes on him. His gaze was cold, as though forged on snow-covered peaks instead of in caverns where primates lit the first bonfires.

'It's not a pleasant story.'

Everardo took three drags from the cigarette and instinctively slowed down, as if wanting to show the stranger that he was in no rush to get him out of the car.

'Go on, tell me. I won't be sleeping tonight anyway, I've got a long way to go and I'll be driving all night . . .'

'You still haven't told me what *you* do.'

'I'm a photographer.'

'A journalist?'

'No . . .' Everardo hesitated. 'I shoot models.'

'An enviable job.'

Jacobo sat back in his seat and crossed his arms. His face took on the same meditative expression it had worn when Everardo picked him up on the side of the road. He went on:

'A week ago, three men went into an almost unexplored network of caves in these mountains. While they were crawling single-file through a narrow passage with barely enough room for their bodies, a huge rock came loose from the roof and broke the back of the man in the middle. He was stuck; his companions found it impossible to move the rock. The guy in the back, I'll call him spelunker number three, backed up and went to get help. The one in front, number one, couldn't get out; the body and the rock blocked his way. After exploring for a short time, he found that there was no way out on his side. After the impact, number two fainted, but when he regained consciousness a few minutes later he started to scream. Number three returned hours later with bad news: the rescuers couldn't reach them. He gave them painkillers and sedatives, but it was no good: number two wouldn't stop howling. Number three came back the first four days to see how they were doing. After that he didn't return again: the stench and the screams were unbearable. Number one only had two choices: wait for his companion to die, or kill him. The only way he could get out of there was by using his pickaxe to break the rock that was crushing his colleague ...'

'Kill him?' Everardo said, shocked. 'I could never do that ...'

'If you really think about it, the second option isn't so crazy: imagine number two's desperation, unable to move, pinned to the ground like a butterfly in a collection. A terrible torture ...'

'And what finally happened?' Everardo threw his cigarette butt out the window and switched on the headlights. The mountains awaited a few miles ahead, silent, indifferent to the drama that had taken place in their depths.

'The ending will have to wait,' said Jacobo. 'Can you stop for a second? I need to pee.'

Everardo pulled over, turned off the engine, and put on his blinkers. As he watched Jacobo disappear behind a tree, he had a sudden impulse: he leaned over into the back seat and quickly rifled through the backpack. His hand touched something cold and sharp; he pulled out a pickaxe and looked at it in the flame from his lighter: the edge was stained with dried blood. He felt a stabbing pain in his stomach and his mind froze for a few seconds; without thinking, he held onto the tool and closed the backpack. Out of the corner of his eye he saw Jacobo's shadow reaching out to open the door. Everardo swiveled around and put his hands on the wheel.

'All done,' the spelunker said, rubbing his hands and sitting down beside him. 'It's getting colder than fuck out there, good thing you picked me up. Ready to go?'

Everardo turned the key to start the van. He felt Jacobo's gaze on him, enveloping him like a blue haze; his eyes were watching him with suspicion.

'You won't tell anybody, right?' the spelunker said at last, after a prolonged silence.

Everardo shook his head. Night had fallen, dissolving the landscape. It was just the two of them and the road.

'I lied to you . . . I do work in a team. Although this time we weren't trying to get a body out, we were just having fun. Ironic, isn't it?'

'I lied to you too: I do work for a newspaper, the crime section, but I'm on vacation now. I understand what you had to do . . .'

The two men looked at one another for a moment in the darkness. Everardo smiled at Jacobo conspiratorially.

'There's something else I haven't told you,' Jacobo said. 'You're thinking, because you saw the blood on the pickaxe, that I'm spelunker number one, but really I'm number three.'

'And the blood?'

'You didn't search the backpack well enough. Spelunker number one's head is inside. He waited until number two died, then got out. But I was outside, waiting for him . . . I never went for the rescuers or brought them painkillers.'

Everardo swallowed hard. His nervous hands tightened on the wheel.

'Why?'

'I could tell you it was for money: they'd been taking advantage of me for years, cheating me out of a fair share of the reward money . . . But really it was just a fit of madness. I didn't plan it, I simply took advantage of the situation.'

'What are you going back for now?'

'You're the one that works on crimes. Didn't they teach you that killers always return to the scene of the crime?'

Everardo sighed. He had one last question:

'What are you going to do with me?'

'Nothing,' answered Jacobo. His voice sounded tired. 'I left the bodies in a very deep cavern. No one will ever be able to verify this story . . . that is, if you dare to tell it.'

Everardo saw how the van's headlights illuminated the gray shadow of the mountains, which were drawing ever closer. Jacobo went on:

'And just think, this could be one of those stories people tell on the road or around a campfire. You never really saw the head in the backpack, and the blood on the pickaxe could be clay and mud. Which version do you prefer?'

After thinking about it, Everardo answered:

'I don't know . . . I suppose it's more interesting meeting a murderer than a liar.'

'Don't knock liars: they're great storytellers. In any case, what you believe says a lot more about you than it does about me. That's the key to every story.'

Outside the van the night grew like a presence. Everardo and Jacobo exchanged a final glance, then focused on the lines on the road. They didn't exchange another word the rest of the trip.

The Dream of the Fisherman's Wife

I've been married to my wife for seven years, but it wasn't until yesterday that I found out about her sleepwalking. I don't know if it's an old condition or a new one. What I do know is that it'll be hard to find out for sure, since my wife and I are hardly talking. We lost trust in each other a long time ago; I sleep in my study, and when we're home at the same time we avoid each other. This new development is the latest in a series of strange behaviors on my wife's part in recent weeks, although I suppose she could say the same thing about me. We're such strangers to each other that even something as simple as watching her chew – on the rare occasions I go in the kitchen and find her having a bite to eat – seems somehow out of place. One day I saw her bent over a plate of watermelon wedges; hearing me come in, Estela sat up and shot me a glance that reminded me of how a predator looks when surprised with its prey. A thread of red juice ran down the corner of her mouth, adding a sinister touch to the scene.

Last night I got thirsty in the middle of the night and left my studio to get a glass of water. As I crossed the living room I saw my wife standing in front of the sliding glass door that leads to the balcony. It was open halfway and the night breeze was moving the curtains, making them ripple over Estela's face. She stood with her back to me, totally still. The movement of the curtains, plus the light of the streetlamp filtering through them, caused a curious effect: it looked like my wife was passing through a curtain of water. I could tell something strange was going on, so I walked up beside her. Her eyes were open, lost in nothingness; she gave me the impression that she was looking at something beyond the waking world. She ignored my presence, so I spoke to her gently. She didn't respond. I stood there waiting for several minutes, until suddenly she said:

'You are the Creator.'

Then she turned around and walked slowly back to her room. I followed her, stopping at the threshold. From there I saw her get between the sheets.

I was stunned at the discovery of her sleepwalking. However, something else disturbed me too, something to do with the phrase she uttered in her sleep.

Estela is an atheist.

I've decided to keep this journal to put my thoughts in order. I want to understand how Estela and I got to this point. At what moment do two people in love lose their way and wind up adrift like the ghosts of their own relationship? I've wondered many times why we didn't split up. I don't have an explanation. Instead of answers, what comes to me are questions: what spell keeps couples together when they no longer have anything in common? Maybe there's an invisible bond, a final stronghold which, in their despair and despondency, crumbling marriages are unable to take advantage of. Married life has many mysteries, but maybe the biggest is when relationships keep going even after they're over. I think what we see in many married couples – my case, of course – is like the light from dead stars: merely the reflection of something extinct.

I'm writing this entry after finding Estela standing facing the balcony for the second night in a row. The same image: the half-open door, the rippling curtains. It didn't go any further, and that reassures me. We live on the first floor; there's barely two meters between us and the street. But it's not a fall

I'm worried about; I'm afraid she'll go out in the street in that condition. Yesterday I locked the door to the balcony, but she still found a way to open it: I guess sleepwalkers are able to perform certain actions.

She stood there motionless for long minutes before finally uttering the same sentence:

'You are the Creator.'

She was looking towards the horizon. When she turned around and walked back to her room, I stepped out onto the balcony. I thought maybe there was something outside that was arousing my wife's strange reveries.

All I saw were the neighbors' darkened windows, like blind eyes unable to return my gaze.

We wanted to have a child.

In all honesty, she much more than me. (I have to be as precise as possible, if I want to make sense of these strange events.) We tried to get pregnant for two years without success. Then we went to the doctor. After a series of tests, the doctor explained that the problem was me. I needed an operation. I refused, arguing to my wife that the doctor was just trying to get more money out of us. The truth is that I was scared: of the operation, of fatherhood. So I clung to the pretext of the money-grubbing doctor to put the subject off as long as possible. Then Estela suggested we get a second opinion. I agreed. There were more tests and the same result: the operating room. My income had dropped around that time, so I used lack of funds as an excuse. We had to be patient and wait for a better time to incur that expense. While we argued about it, another year went by. The worst year of our marriage, which culminated in my sleeping in the study and Estela talking in her sleep.

Now I know what I have to do. We've ignored each other so long that the idea of spying on her hadn't even occurred to me. I don't mean following her in the car or showing up unannounced at her office. In the morning, when she goes to work, I'll rummage through her drawers. I'll search her closet. I'll even switch on her computer. I know her password; I doubt she's changed it in years. I need to find something that explains her behavior.

Maybe, deep down, what I'm looking for is a reason to leave her for good.

I'm picking up this journal again after three days of investigation. Days in which, by the way, my wife hasn't given up her ritual of the balcony and uttering the sentence which at this point sends chills up my spine. The search yielded results. Or at least I think so. Because what I've found out doesn't really lead me anywhere. It's something that makes no sense, no matter how hard I try to understand it. Maybe Estela and I are going crazy together, in a final and desperate act of love.

My wife has been obsessed for some time with an image. It's a woodcut from the early 19th century, the work of the Japanese artist Katsushika Hokusai. I know because I found a file about it in one of her desk drawers. And on her computer I was able to find a series of searches about it, dating back months. She even tried buying a reproduction being sold by a gallery in New York, but apparently the deal fell through. Although I'm not sure. Is it possible she has that picture somewhere in the house? I've looked all over but haven't found it. Just the thought of that repulsive art being hidden in my own home infuriates me.

The picture is disgusting. Worthy of a twisted, vulgar mind.

The Dream of the Fisherman's Wife depicts a naked woman lying down while a gigantic octopus performs cunnilingus on her. The animal's black, bulging eyes as it opens its mouth are frightening, but the most disturbing part of the picture is the woman's expression. However grotesque the scene may appear, she feels an intense pleasure, as if no human could equal the octopus as a lover, for the creature also caresses her entire body with its tentacles.

What does all this have to do with my wife's sleepwalking? That picture Estela seems to adore is bona fide proof that I've been living with a woman I don't know. However much I thought I knew about her private life, now she reveals herself to me as a creature with voracious, inhuman eyes.

Just like the octopus in the picture.

Finding the picture became an obsession.

I was convinced that Estela was keeping it in some nook or cranny of the house. I checked her closet again. I opened the boxes she stores in the garage. I even searched her car. Nothing. It didn't surprise me: if a woman could conceal her true personality from her husband, she was capable of hiding anything. These sorts of paranoid thoughts have sprouted in my head the past few days and reinforced my determination to find the picture. If I managed to locate it, it would be a small victory in the midst of so much deception.

Later I thought about it and decided I was being too hard on Estela, the woman I had loved for many years. And I let a new idea take root in my mind: my wife was talking to me in her sleep; the way she was acting, getting up every night – and uttering those words, meaningless to someone who doesn't believe in God – was a prayer directed to me, an attempt from the deepest part of her consciousness to raise my spirits and reassure me that I was capable of getting her pregnant. I was almost convinced that the 'Creator' she referred to in her nocturnal mantra was me, when something happened that brought me back to reality.

I found the picture. She was hiding it in a place so obvious that it escaped my suspicions for that very reason.

It was morning. Estela had just left for work, and you could still catch a trace of her perfume in the house. It smelled as though she had changed scents, and I went into her room to look for the bottle. Any little detail might mean a clue amid all that absurdity. Suddenly something caught my attention. I had seen it out of the corner of my eye, something black and pointy somewhere on the bed. I turned towards the bed with a knot in my stomach. The corner of a frame was sticking out from under the pillow. I went closer and with a trembling hand pulled out the woodcut.

There it was, the abominable image, lying underneath where she rested her head every night, whispering who knew what things into her ear, into the mind she'd already lost. The revelation of such an act was dreadful, unacceptable.

What kind of person lets a monster lull her to sleep?

Despite the events of the past few days, I wasn't ready for what happened in the middle of the night. I haven't slept much lately. The routine of keeping an eye on what Estela is doing at night, and following her tracks during the day, has left little room for sleep. However, last night I fell asleep reading in my study. The built-up fatigue finally overtook me. It was a deep sleep, which kept me knocked out until dawn. I awoke as the sky was starting to get light. I got up immediately, seized with panic: I hadn't been awake to monitor my wife's sleepwalking. I looked for her all over the house but couldn't find her. The balcony door was wide open, making me fear the worst. I ran to the front door, ready to search for her in the streets. When I opened it, I got a surprise: Estela was there, her eyes open, lost somewhere in dreamland. I hugged her, relieved, and then noticed something I'd missed: her dress was soaked, as if she'd just gotten out of a pool. I pulled it aside to look at her.

What I saw has brought my insomnia back.

Estela had a series of slimy green residues in her hair and on her shoulders. I took a piece of it between my fingers.

It was seaweed.

*

This city isn't by the sea. I'm clarifying that so you can understand, in some way, what I have left to tell. I'll admit it was an act of desperation, but what other choice is left when your reality comes to seem like a nightmare? The only place where Estela could swim through seaweed was the Aquarium. After thinking it over a long time, I decided to visit it in the late afternoon, when there are fewer people there.

I bought a ticket and walked like a robot through the blue passageways. I realized I was copying my wife. I hardly looked at the enormous glass cases, as if my steps knew where to lead me. I remember how the reflection of the water created the sensation of movement on the floor and the walls; how the creatures I saw swimming out of the corner of my eye seemed to be approaching the glass to watch me.

It was like I was really walking on the ocean floor, through a passage separating me from an even deeper abyss.

Then I was there, in front of him. Clearly he was waiting for me. In the final display case, occupying a tank all by himself, floating, majestic . . .

His tentacles unfolded in the water as if they wanted to embrace me.

I haven't left the study in days. My appetite is gone, along with any desire to clean myself up. I'm afraid to face my wife. To look at her and discover the arrogant look of victory on her face. I can tell she has stopped sleepwalking. From here I hear her coming and going confidently through the house, the cadence of steps that have recovered their rhythm.

I wonder if that means the end of the nightmare . . . or only the beginning.

Estela leaves no room for speculation and slips something under the door. I stand up, falteringly. I hesitate, then finally bend over to pick the object up with a trembling hand.

It's a pregnancy test.

The Paradoxical Man

I

'When did the nightmares start?'

'A month ago.'

'That's a long time. You must be exhausted.'

'Really I'm more worried than exhausted.'

'I can help you. Psychoanalysis will ease your mind.'

'I need you to be honest with me. Will my creative process be affected by the therapy?'

'Definitely. Your psyche will readjust how it perceives the world. The idea is for it to interpret the things around you in a way that's less disturbing.'

'Then I can't accept your help.'

'Are you sure?'

'I'm loyal to my obsessions. If that means continuing with the nightmares, I'm afraid I'll have to go on dreaming them.'

II

J. Crowley showed up ten minutes early for his rendezvous. He went through the red curtains and into the small, crowded bar. He found a seat at the bar and ordered coffee: he needed something to wake him up. He glanced around the dimly lit place; as usual, he didn't recognize a single face. He'd been coming to this bar for years and the clientele seemed to change every night.

He was on his second coffee when Bela arrived. He sat down on a stool beside him and ordered a gin. His friend pointed a long finger at the steaming mug.

'Still having the nightmares?'

J. Crowley took a sip of his beverage and nodded.

'I decided not to do the therapy. It might affect my writing.'

The bartender set the gin on the bar along with a dish of sunflower seeds.

'Are you writing?' asked Bela. 'You have that look you get when you can't concentrate.'

'What look?'

Bela took a handful of sunflower seeds.

'The one that says: "I'd kill for a good idea." '

J. Crowley pushed the half-full cup of coffee away.

'I won't lie to you. I'm in a bind: therapy isn't an option, but at the same time, these dreams have started to mess with my work rhythm. I don't know what to do . . .'

Bela swallowed the seeds with a gulp of gin, as if they were medicine. Then he reached into his inner coat pocket and pulled out a card.

'What's this?' J. Crowley hesitated before taking it.

'Consider it an *alternative* therapy. My wife often goes to them, she says they're really good.'

'What's it consist of?'

Bela motioned to the bartender for another gin.

'I don't know. All my wife told me is that it has to do with books. With *literature*, I mean. So I thought it might work for you . . .'

J. Crowley read the card. For a moment he thought his friend was playing a joke on him, but he knew he was incapable of making fun of him, much less at a time like the one he was going through.

The card had a phone number for scheduling an appointment and a name that caught his attention:

'The Order of the Crow'.

III

Resistance was futile. Sooner or later sleep would overtake him, and then the nightmares wasted no time in coming, as they did that night. The scenes changed: immense precipices whose bottom he couldn't see, endless fields full of dried-up, twisted trees, an ancient city that was apparently deserted but whose inhabitants you could sense behind the boarded-up windows. However, there was one element that was always present. It was an anthropomorphic figure that seemed to be made of petrified lava. None of its human features could be made out clearly except for one arm – a claw, really – that stretched out from its craggy form with its palm extended as if demanding payment of a tribute.

J. Crowley tried to flee this presence but was unable to. The strange and menacing creature was everywhere. It was a ubiquitous being that overwhelmed him, snatching away the air he breathed. Even though the settings for the nightmares were always boundless landscapes, J. Crowley had the constant sensation that there wasn't enough room for both of them, and therefore that he had to leave. He would wake up in a sweating panic when the creature increased in size to the point of squashing him, giving him no chance of escape. The most terrifying part of J. Crowley's nightmare was the certainty that there was nowhere to run. If that was the world he lived in, where else was he supposed to go? But the presence told him otherwise. Although it never spoke, the message was clear: You don't belong here. Get out.

The worst part was that J. Crowley began feeling the same way even when he was awake. As the day passed, a sense of foreignness grew in him, as though he were an alien exiled on planet Earth. Everyday objects started to give off a ghostly glow. He felt that if he tried to touch them, his fingers would go right through them.

Maybe the creature in his dreams was right. He was an outcast. And the only place he could return to was the Void.

IV

The person who greeted him was an old man who looked like a librarian. He was dressed in a checkered suit and bowtie. They sat down at an enormous oak desk to drink tea. The walls around them were covered with shelves of books. J. Crowley noted that they were hardcover volumes and that everything around him looked neat and orderly, even the Librarian's fingernails, which showed obvious signs of being manicured.

J. Crowley described his nightmares at length and without interruptions. When he finished, the Librarian adjusted his bowtie, which had shifted a little to one side, and cleared his throat before speaking.

'Before I tell you what I think, I have to explain something. We are an Order that bases its knowledge on the contents of certain books. For us, authors like Edgar Allan Poe, H. P. Lovecraft, and Arthur Machen were visionaries who could see into other worlds that exist within our own. Most people consider their works mere fiction, but for the Order they are absolute truths. We use them to interpret and provide guidance on the inexplicable events that affect our patients, most of whom are so desperate that they submit to our peculiar method even though at first they don't believe us. But you're different. You're a Creator, like them. So you can understand what I'm saying better than anyone.'

J. Crowley looked at the bottom of his empty teacup. He didn't know how to reply. He was uneasy about putting himself in the hands of this kindly man who seemed trapped in the nineteenth century, but at the same time he was intrigued by his method. After a few seconds, he looked up and met the Librarian's gaze. His look was transparent, like the surface of a lake that shows you its bottom and invites you to immerse yourself in it.

'Of course I understand,' he said, nodding. 'How can you help me?'

The Librarian smiled, satisfied. He got up from the desk, went straight to one of the shelves, and returned with a book which he examined with a look of concentration.

'From what you've told me, I'm confident that the presence that has been manifesting in your dreams is Cynothoglys. It's an ancient deity described by Thomas Ligotti in his story "The Prodigy of Dreams".'

'What does this deity represent?' J. Crowley asked with growing interest.

The Librarian proceeded to read solemnly from the book:

'It is a god without shape, the god of changes and confusion, the god of decomposition, the god that buries gods as well as men, the one that kills and buries all things.'

J. Crowley shifted in the chair, uneasy.

'And what does he want from me?'

The Librarian closed the book.

'It's extremely rare for Cynothoglys to appear,' he said, after a few moments' reflection. 'And when he does, it's for a very particular reason . . .'

'What reason?' J. Crowley asked anxiously.

'Before I give you a definitive diagnosis,' the Librarian replied, 'I'd like to consult with my colleagues about your case. I hope you don't mind.'

J. Crowley was about to object, but checked himself. The Librarian had skillfully led him to a fantasy world, strung him along. Now it was time to return to the real world.

★

V

It was the worst nightmare in weeks.

As if the creature the Librarian had identified as Cynotho-glys were angered by his actions, J. Crowley had a dream from which he woke up screaming. Surrounded by the darkness of his bedroom, he brought both hands to his chest in an attempt to stop his heart from pounding. Unlike the previous dreams, this one was not characterized by bleak landscapes, nor did it evoke a constant sense of danger. This time Cynothoglys approached in a *friendly* way, in a manner of speaking. The creature led him through well-known streets to the outskirts of the city. There they climbed a path leading to a hilltop, from which the whole city could be seen. *His* city, the one he had lived in since the day he was born. The view was per-fect. You could make out all the houses, buildings, and parks. Then J. Crowley felt the need to pinpoint his own house. He began to look for it with a certain amount of anxiety, until he found his street, where he could recognize his neighbors' houses, even the trees planted along the sidewalks, but not his own home. Where it should have been, between a black metal fence and a convenience store, there was a vacant lot. At first he thought he must have the wrong street, but after a careful reexamination of the area there could be no doubt. In fact, he could see his neighbor's son playing in the road with that stupid ball that was constantly smacking into his kitchen window. Except now the ball just landed on the empty lot, from which the boy retrieved it after jumping over a fence. And it was at that moment that J. Crowley felt the profound terror that the nightmare embodied.

Cynothoglys was proving to him that he belonged to the Void.

★

VI

After the terrifying dream, J. Crowley had no further hesitation about returning to the Librarian. He had become one of those tortured souls who will accept any help, no matter how absurd. However, given the circumstances of what he was going through now, choosing the Librarian was starting to make sense. While the psychiatrist had warned him that his writing would be affected if he followed his treatment, the Order offered him a way out that was based on books.

This time the Librarian poured him a cognac, which made him assume that it wasn't good news.

'Conferring with my colleagues has confirmed my suspicions.' The Librarian got straight to the point.

'About Cynothoglys?'

'No. I was sure about that . . .'

'Well, then?'

The Librarian took a sip. J. Crowley imitated him.

'Cynothoglys is associated with an extremely rare phenomenon,' the Librarian said, 'which we in the Order call the Paradox. This is the first time we've witnessed it, although there are other, older members who heard it spoken of when they were young.'

J. Crowley took the bottle sitting on the desk and poured himself some more cognac.

'In the world of literature,' the Librarian continued, 'we all know that there must first be an author. An author who writes and creates a body of work over the course of his lifetime. However, there are rare occasions when, due to this Paradox, the exact opposite occurs. That is, that first there is a Work, a literary creation that is an entity in itself, and which in turn feels the need to create an author to serve as its *façade*, you might say. My colleagues and I are convinced that you embody this Paradox.'

J. Crowley set his empty cup on the desk and leaned back in the chair, despondent.

'You realize what you're telling me? That I don't exist . . .'

'I'm afraid that's not the worst part.'

The Librarian took the bottle, filled both cups, and noticed with dismay that the liquor was almost gone.

'The real problem is Cynothoglys,' he continued. 'As a burying deity, he is in charge of fixing the *glitches*. Although it may seem strange, the supernatural world doesn't tolerate imperfections ... imperfections within its own logic. And you're an anomaly within the anomaly. Sort of like a black rectangle within the blackness itself.'

'So Cynothoglys is coming for me.'

The Librarian fixed his eyes on him, and nodded in silence.

'And is there anything that can be done?' J. Crowley asked, almost with resignation.

'There's only one possibility. Maybe the Work that created you hasn't finished writing yet. So go home. Try to get ahead of the Work and put all this on paper. If you can do it, maybe you can separate yourself from the Work, become a person in your own right.'

J. Crowley shifted his gaze to one of the windows. He saw a tree swaying in the wind, a huge black bird perched on one of its branches. It was a simple image, but he wondered if he would be able to describe it.

'And what if I can't do it?' he asked after a long silence. 'What will happen if I sit down to write, but it turns out that the story has already been completed by the Work?'

The Librarian shivered, as if an invisible, icy hand had suddenly brushed the back of his neck.

'Then Cynothoglys will finish his work. And you will disappear before you're able to put the final perio

Leprosy in the Walls

For many years my family celebrated Christmas at the big house in Desierto de los Leones. It was built over a ravine in the early '70s and had three floors: the upper one, where my aunt and uncle and cousins had their bedrooms, the middle one, where the living room, dining room, breakfast nook, and kitchen were located, and the lower floor, a mixed area for recreation and work: a crescent-shaped space around a fireplace, a wet bar, and a study with green carpet and wood paneling where my uncle, who was an accountant, would shut himself up to review invoices. A sliding glass door led out to the back yard, which offered a pleasant view of the ravine. A spiral staircase went down to the final and strangest part of the house: a triangle-shaped part of the property unused by the architect, where there was nothing but a chain-link fence and overgrown grass that swallowed any balls that landed there.

I spent long stretches of my childhood and adolescence in that house, which over time became part of my own mythology; when I grew up, it filled my dreams with images as puzzling as they were disturbing. Whenever I had summer or winter break I would travel from Guadalajara to the Federal District to stay in the guest room and play all day with my cousins: football, *Dungeons & Dragons* on Playstation, hide-and-seek, whatever came to mind. We listened to music too; I remember with a mixture of nostalgia and shame how we took turns kissing Olivia Newton-John's face on the cover of her *Vaseline* album. Best of all was dinnertime; the two live-in servants made delicious garnachas: sopes, gorditas, or quesadillas with molcajete salsa on the side. In Guadalajara I had to fix my own snacks, so a feast like that made me feel like a guest in a hotel. Another of the house's special features was a service staircase running in a spiral from the rooftop terrace to the yard and which we used like a secret passage in the games we invented.

Years later, as we drank beer and remembered the old times in a bar in downtown Tlalpan, my cousin Claudio told me some things I didn't know about the house in Desierto de los Leones and the grounds it was built on. He told me that in the years after the Revolution, the area around the ravine was a seedy place where brothels and casinos flourished, the haunts of thieves, highwaymen, and murderers. That there had been a lot of pain and death in those parts, a lot of bloodshed.

After setting his bottle down on the table he added, with a chilling casualness:

'That's why there were Subhumans and Fleshless in my house.'

His confession threw me. I've never seen anything other-worldly before, but I know – as the famous line from *Hamlet* goes – that 'there are more things in heaven and earth than are dreamt of . . .' Besides, I'm a horror writer. I live off frightening other people. My childhood home was haunted, and I was only just finding out about it.

As was usually the case in my life, whenever anything important happened, I was always last on the scene.

It's no coincidence that I'm remembering all this now. It's December 24 and I'm getting ready to return, for the last time, to the house in Desierto de los Leones. The property was sold. Soon they'll be tearing it down to build an enormous high-rise apartment building. My aunt and uncle, who have lived in Cuernavaca for years, invited the family over for Christmas like in the old days, as a way of saying goodbye. I do the math and realize I haven't set foot in the house in over a

decade, which gives me mixed feelings. It will be my first and
last time going in it since I found out that it's haunted. I'm
excited and terrified at the same time. But it's not ghosts I'm
afraid of. There's something even more disturbing inside the
house at Desierto de los Leones: happy memories. I'm fifty,
with two divorces behind me and a literary career that's never
taken off. I don't know how I'll feel when I walk through the
huge wooden front door. Probably like just another one of
the ghosts that inhabit it.

I'm scared I won't want to leave.

I look at myself in the bathroom mirror as I trim my beard
and my reflection gives me a painful thought: *Maybe you never
did leave, Bernardo*.

I was always the last to everything because I'm the youngest of seven brothers. I was the last to go to university, get
married, have kids. As a child I'd watch my brothers playing
football in the street from my bedroom window. I attended
their weddings as ring bearer and drank soft drinks while
I watched the other guests get drunk. I grew up with a rift
in time and space: the best things always happened to other
people, in other places. That's why I made the house at Desierto de los Leones my own, a place where I had cousins my
own age. My parents were aware of the issue and let me stay
there for weeks at a time. They felt guilty for having me so
many years after my next oldest brother. I was what people
in those days called a 'bonus': one last, unplanned child. My
brothers changed my diapers and scolded me; I had many
parents, but no playmates.

I grew up like a ghost in my own house.

Now I have to tell about the cave incident.

The ravine by the Desierto de los Leones house led to a
small valley, which was crossed by a stream. At the end of that
valley rose a hill with a single street and three houses. On one
side of this nascent housing development were three caverns:

tunnels left behind from an old sand mine. You could make them out clearly from the balcony in the TV room. My cousins and I liked to spend long periods looking at them while imagining what might be inside.

One morning in early December, when the winter weather was starting to set in, Claudio issued the challenge:

'Come on, let's go to the caves. Don't be sissies.'

Besides my cousins there were a couple of their friends. They all got excited. I refused: in the first place I was scared, and besides I thought the proper place for adventures was in your imagination. I thought so then, and I still think so now. I feigned a stomachache and stayed home. The group set out after lunch. I followed their progress from the balcony, saw them jump over the triangular fence in the second garden, then venture into the trees. Left behind, there was nothing for me to do but sit and watch a game show. As it grew darker outside, I regretted not having gone with them. I was a coward.

My cousins and their friends returned four hours later, in time for dinner. They were hungry and exhausted, their clothes and faces stained with mud. Getting there had been an adventure, they told me as they devoured one sope after another. Their story was full of details about the obstacles they'd had to overcome: the stream which had suddenly gotten too wide, some wild dogs that chased them through the valley, the climb up the rock-covered hill. On the other hand, the caverns had turned out not to be too exciting. All they found there were rusty tools, rotting ropes, a homeless person's filthy mattress. They hadn't stayed very long because the sun was starting to set.

After dinner, the friends said goodbye and my cousins and I went to play Playstation. Later, when I was about to fall asleep, Claudio came into the guest room, sat down on the bed beside me, and told me something that had happened in the caves.

'Swear you won't tell anybody,' he insisted.

'I swear,' I answered, intrigued.

He told me that he had been the one to go furthest in exploring the caverns. He discovered they were connected. He didn't have a flashlight: he lit his way using a lighter flame, which he had to put out every time it got hot because it burned his fingers. As a result he got disoriented; he was lost for several minutes, passing from one tunnel to another without finding the exit. At some point he saw a figure coming towards him; he thought it was one of his companions. When it was right in front of him, he beheld something that surprised him: it was me.

'I thought you ended up feeling better and caught up with us,' Claudio said.

In the lighter's weak glow, my cousin realized something else.

'It was you,' he added. 'But older: you had a beard.'

A gust of air blew out the lighter flame. When he lit it again, there was nobody in front of him.

My cousin managed to get out of the caves and didn't mention the incident to anybody.

'What do you think it could have been?' I asked him in a trembling voice.

Claudio got up from the bed, headed to the bedroom door, and stood in the doorway, thinking. Before he left, he said:

'There are only two possibilities: either I'm crazy or I saw your double.'

Both were unsettling. That night I slept with the light on.

In the olden days they had a particular way of referring to haunted houses. There's a section in the Bible in the Book of Leviticus, a law that considered that homes could be infected, just like people's skin or their garments. It was called 'leprosy in the walls'. When this happened, the priest had to enter the house and examine the blemishes on the walls. 'If he observes greenish or reddish depressions in the walls,' say verses 37-38, 'then he shall go outside, through the door of the house, and close it up for seven days.' There was an exorcism that went with the ritual: two birds were brought to the house, one of them was sacrificed and its blood sprinkled on the affected walls. Afterwards the living bird would be set free outside the town, in the countryside. 'In this way he will make atonement for the house, and it will be clean.' A modern-day interpretation might connect such spots with moisture or mold; however, I still think it's interesting that a haunted house was thought of like a living being suffering from a disease.

The house at Desierto de los Leones had its own intervention. That time in the bar in Tlalpan, Claudio told me that he had brought a medium there to perform a cleansing. The woman lit candles and incense; she said prayers. She was the one who told him there were Subhumans and Fleshless, esoteric terms for demons and ghosts. What had been the result of the medium's visit? Strange things happened in the house, attested to by my cousin as well as the servants: vases that went flying through the air and shattered on the floor, objects that were lost and never found again, echoes of conversations that grew louder in the middle of the night. And, above all, a presence that lurked in a corner of the breakfast nook, where an inexplicable cold was often felt, accompanied by the glimpse of a silhouette out of the corner of one's eye. The servants described it as an old man wearing a hat.

After the cleansing, the Subhumans vanished. The old man – the Fleshless – remained, until the night Claudio decided to confront him.

The house at Desierto de los Leones appears constantly in my dreams. In them its interior is much larger than in real life, and times are usually mixed together: I see myself in shorts, playing with a ball or drinking wine with one of my ex-wives. In the dream that recurs most often I'm an adult. I'm walking alone down the spiral staircase that leads to the lower floor, where the servants' quarters are, and a door leading out to the yard. But instead of the room where the servants sleep, there's a huge, dark hallway, a tunnel crossing the house from one side to the other. I explore this passage, where there's nothing but a thick blackness and moisture emanating from the walls. I know that I'm in the house and at the same time somewhere else. A threshold or a portal – a womb, maybe. I walk as a growing feeling of anxiety takes hold of me. The tunnel seems to have no end, and the unease stems from a certainty: there's no turning back. I have to keep going. There's something on the other side, a place I have to go because a presence is waiting for me. The most disconcerting thing is that I never get there. I wake up every time with the unpleasant feeling that part of me stayed behind in that dream, and that I won't get it back until that knowledge – denied to me for now – is finally revealed.

My cousin Claudio is a musician. When his parents left to live in Cuernavaca, he turned the study on the lower floor into a recording booth. He lives off doing jingles. Back then he used to play nights in a bar with his rock group, and when he came home he'd shut the door and work for a couple of hours; that helped him burn off the adrenaline and get to sleep. Once in the middle of the night while he was composing the tune for a gastritis medicine, he took a break to go up to the kitchen for a snack. As he passed the breakfast area, he felt the presence of the Fleshless: the hairs on the back of his neck stood up; he was engulfed in a sudden, sticky cold, as if he'd just put on a wet sweater. He remembered the medium's advice and decided to confront it. YOU'RE NOT WELCOME, he shouted. GET OUT OF HERE. And he recited a prayer the medium had taught him. After a tense silence, he went back to the recording booth.

A few minutes later he started to hear a strange noise. At

first he thought it was interference, a sound coming through the headphones. But when he took them off, he realized the noise was still there. He looked around and what he discovered left him stunned: a cascade of water was rushing through the ceiling of the studio and flowing down one of the walls. Alarmed, he climbed the stairs, where he found more water; he had to splash his way up to the next floor. The breakfast nook was flooded. The water came up to his ankles. Claudio felt overwhelmed by this unexpected and urgent situation. After a few seconds of paralysis he went into action, looking for the source of the problem. He found it in the kitchen: the sink pipe had burst. He found the shutoff valve and turned it off. He had to wake up his brothers to help get rid of the accumulated water. Dawn found them finishing drying the floor.

'Nothing like that had ever happened before,' Claudio told me in the bar in Tlalpan. 'Not even a drip.'

A huge coincidence: after confronting the Fleshless, the only flood in the house's forty years of existence occurred. But Claudio and I knew that nothing happened by chance.

'What happened with the ghost?' I asked.

My cousin took a long swig of his beer.

'We never felt him again,' he said. 'After that night, he disappeared.'

The dead of night. Dinner is almost finished. The menu was an homage to all our family Christmases: turkey, cod, pork shanks, *romeritos*, apple salad, a lot of wine. I listen to the conversations, the laughter coming from the dining room, while I stumble – the effects of the alcohol – down the stairs leading to the lower floor of the house. Earlier I took the time to explore it. The parquet floor is swollen and uneven in several sections. The walls peeling and moisture-stained. The carpet threadbare and dirty. I find the house's deterioration unbearable. It looks more like the place from my dreams than the one in my childhood memories.

If we were in biblical times, the priests would consider it a haunted place. For me it is: the leprosy of the past.

There are still a few objects remaining, which my aunt and uncle were giving away during dinner to interested family members: lamps, bookcases, tables. They have a month to remove what's left before the heavy machinery begins the demolition process. Bulldozers and cranes that will pulverize the place containing my family's memories. I think that everything that has happened in the house will not be destroyed: it will be let loose like a Pandora's box.

I open the sliding glass door to the back yard. The icy wind from the ravine hits my face, reviving me. I discover what I already knew: that the valley had vanished to make way for a concrete expressway that runs under the house and connects the upper level of the beltway with Santa Fe. It's called Avenida de los Poetas. The hill on the other side is still there, although now there are more buildings and streets.

I've always arrived late to everything. A punishment when it comes to good things, but also a blessing with the bad. I don't know what awaits me on this occasion. I step into the yard and head toward the stairs going down to the triangle of overgrown grass, to the furthest part of the grounds. I stop on the first step. I feel the house's presence behind me, that dying entity that seems to loom over me, pushing me to go on. I won't turn back: just like in my dream, I know that I have to keep going.

I peer at the horizon. The caves are still there on the hill, with their black maws, waiting for the moment to swallow me.

Señor Ligotti

S eñor Ligotti showed up at the end of a conference. As usual, Esteban signed some books, listened to his readers with studied politeness and gave quick, concise tips to the ones aspiring to become writers. When he was preparing to leave the auditorium, with that mixture of satisfaction and emptiness he felt after every presentation – yes, he had readers, but he always wanted more – he saw him sitting in the back row, with his red canvas bag, the bowtie in place of a necktie, the snow-white beard, the tips of his mustache ending in points in the style of some figures from the Revolution, and a walking stick with a silver-plated handle.

Señor Ligotti rose to his feet with a surprising agility, shook his hand vigorously – Esteban could feel the hardness of several rings pressing against his skin – and got straight to the point.

'I'd like to make you a business proposition. Can I buy you a coffee?'

Normally Esteban would have refused. He didn't like chatting with people from the audience beyond what was necessary; talking with strangers made him uncomfortable. He often received invitations to workshops, reading groups, and even bars, which he rejected while trying to hide his irritation. This time he had the perfect excuse: his wife was about to give birth and he had to get home as soon as possible. Maybe that's what made him accept, the need to distract himself from the stress of the imminent childbirth, from the anxiety that didn't let him concentrate to read or write.

Esteban soon found himself sitting in a booth at a Vips cafeteria with this elderly eccentric, who seemed plucked off a theater stage and who at the same time had an impeccable bearing and an overwhelming dignity. Esteban was hanging out with a stranger. *Having kids changes you* was a phrase he'd gotten used to hearing since Adela had gotten pregnant.

Señor Ligotti stared at him with a worried look.

'How are things going for you? Do writers make a good living?'

A typical question. Before answering, Esteban glanced at the book display stands next to the cash register, filled with bestsellers. Every time he went in a Vips, he lamented that his novels weren't part of that club: the books that were sold in bookstores, but also in supermarkets, shops, restaurants.

'I make a living from my writing, but it could be better.'

'For all of us it could be better. Worse too. It's all about knowing how to take advantage of opportunities. Do you own your own home?'

'No. No matter how much I save, I never have enough.'

Señor Ligotti took a sip of his coffee and set it back down on the table. Then he moved his ring-filled fingers, making them chime against the mug.

'Si non oscillas, noli tintinnare . . .'

'What?'

'It's an old saying, as old as I am. If you don't swing, you don't ring, like bells. I've been one of your readers for a long time: I think you're a talented writer who deserves better luck. I know you're obsessed with the Colonia Juárez neighborhood, since many of your stories take place there. I own an apartment in the Berlín building, which I'm putting up for sale. Are you interested?'

Esteban looked at his beer: he had hardly touched it. Meanwhile Señor Ligotti was on his third coffee. Maybe he didn't sleep?

'I've rented my whole life. I've always dreamt of buying a house . . .'

'How much do you have?'

'Not even a million pesos.'

Señor Ligotti stroked his beard with his ring-laden hand. The one on his pinky finger had the National University logo: a shield borne by two birds of prey.

'Give me what you have and it's yours. I'd rather that someone who values old buildings live there and care for it. I'm very fond of that apartment.'

Señor Ligotti's eyes glazed over. He paused to let out a long sigh.

'I lived there with my wife. She died last year.'

'I'm sorry.'

'The money isn't an issue for me. It's a sentimental thing: I can't leave all those memories to just anyone.'

The old man stood up and placed a card on the table. Before leaving, he said:

'Come and see me at my office. And bring your lawyer, if that makes you feel more comfortable.'

Esteban was thoughtful. It was the kind of offer he fantasized about getting, but he didn't want to take advantage of a melancholy old man. He looked out the window: a luxury car pulled up to collect Señor Ligotti. The chauffeur got out and opened the back door for him.

Esteban went to the cash register. The bill had already been paid.

Adela was suspicious. Sitting at the kitchen table, her hands on her belly to feel the baby when it moved, she had listened to Esteban's story as he paced back and forth, increasingly euphoric. She told him to be cautious. Things didn't happen so easily. Not to them. Nor did she believe in coincidences. Everything had a reason, a consequence.

'It smells like fraud.'

Esteban opened the refrigerator. He looked inside, took out a slice of ham and closed it again.

'Why would a rich old man commit a fraud? It's absurd.'

'We don't know anything about him. He could be a decoy, the tip of the iceberg of something we can't even imagine.'

'Do you hear yourself? We should write a suspense novel together. You're more paranoid than I am.'

'I'm suspicious, which is different. And more intuitive than you. Let's suppose he really is a rich, lonely widower. An eccentric man who commits frauds in order to . . .'

'In order to what?'

'. . . amuse himself.'

Esteban knelt down beside Adela. He put his hands on her belly in an attempt to reassure her.

'Some of our friends have had opportunities like this, somebody who gave them a good deal. And we always say, "They're so lucky!" Well, now it's our turn. Don't they say that babies bring good luck?'

'That money is all we have. And we're on the verge of becoming parents. At least bring a lawyer to the meeting, someone to advise you.'

'Lawyers are expensive. I have experience with contracts, remember that I've signed lots of them for my books. Trust me.'

Adela felt exhausted. For eight months she'd had something living inside her that she couldn't see but that she could feel moving within her, growing, feeding. She slept little and badly. She didn't want to go on arguing; she got up and went silently to bed.

Esteban remained in the kitchen. He looked out the window into the pitch-dark night, barely illuminated by the poor lighting of Colonia Juárez.

Somewhere in the midst of all that darkness was their new home, waiting for them.

*

Esteban walked into the lobby of a luxurious building that housed various offices. He saw from the wall directory that the office of Ligotti Industries shared a floor with the corporate offices of Grau Press, an important transnational imprint that had rejected his work on several occasions. That coincidence upset him, stirring up old frustrations. What was so bad about his writing that it was unworthy of being included in their catalog? Grau Press published renowned authors, but also a lot of rubbish. Esteban didn't fool himself: he knew he'd never win a prestigious literary award – he wrote thrillers, a genre scorned by critics – but at the same time he knew that his books had merit. And what's more, they sold. So what was the problem? That's what he was thinking as he stepped off the elevator on the top floor, and he was still turning it over in his mind when, after a short wait, the secretary told him to go in.

Señor Ligotti's office impressed him: marble floor, mahogany furniture, leather chairs, cut glass ashtrays, and books: the walls were covered with shelves. As he sat down in front of the desk and Señor Ligotti handed him the sale contract to review, he noticed that a large part of that library consisted of Grau Press titles. Curiosity got the better of him and he asked his host why.

'I know the owner, we're good friends. Every time a new title comes out, he gives me a copy. By the way, you should publish with them: they're an important publishing house, it would get your name out there.'

'I've tried, but I haven't had any luck.'

'Talent isn't a question of luck. It's all about getting a push in the right direction. I can help you.'

Esteban's eyes shone with intensity. He started flipping through the pages of the contract and signed them without paying any attention.

'Really? I wouldn't dream of asking you for that favor . . .'

Señor Ligotti moved his ring-laden fingers over the glass

ashtray, producing a sound similar to the one he had made with the mug at Vips. For a moment, Esteban felt that time had stopped, that nothing else existed but that rhythmic, hypnotic tapping.

Si non oscillas, noli tintinnare.

Señor Ligotti's voice brought him back to reality.

'You're not asking, I'm offering. It's in your best interest: several of the titles you see here were published thanks to my timely intervention. And with great success. I have a good eye, my neighbor knows it.'

'I should sit down to write. Lately things haven't been easy for me. Pregnancy comes with a lot of worries and complications. For example . . .'

He was on the point of affixing his signature to the final page, but Señor Ligotti interrupted him:

'Wait. Before we finish with this, I'd like us to make a verbal pact, a gentleman's agreement.'

Esteban's mind was still full of the worries he hadn't managed to express: diapers, ultrasounds, the birth.

'Yes?'

The old man was now holding his cane in his hands and stroking the silver handle. When had he picked it up?

'That you let me visit you in the apartment. It's the only condition I impose. We can talk about books, drink coffee, and discuss the progress of the work I'll be pitching to Grau Press.'

Esteban smiled, relieved. For a moment he had thought the deal was going to slip through his fingers.

'Of course.'

He signed, sealing the pact.

The move took place a week later. To celebrate, Esteban threw a party and invited his writer friends and some ex-colleagues from when he used to work in the cultural bureaucracy. He drank one beer after another as he showed the flat to each guest who arrived. The Berlín building was an old edifice, well maintained. Just the type of place he liked. The apartment had high ceilings, thick walls, hardwood flooring. Three bedrooms, two full baths. There was a fireplace in the living room, which gave it a touch of elegance. And the best part: it was on the ground floor, which would save him from having to climb the stairs with the stroller.

At some point that night he was approached by Clemente, an author of crime novels whom he'd known for many years and with whom he had the kind of friendship that usually develops between writers: disingenuous, self-serving, based more on gossip than a genuine interest in each other's work.

Clemente was drinking mezcal from a mug; there weren't enough glasses.

'This apartment is amazing. How did you manage to pay for it?'

'I got a loan. Going into debt is the only way.'

'And the down payment? Through the roof, I'm guessing.'

'My mother-in-law helped us.'

'And how are the neighbors? Have you gone to ask them for sugar?'

Esteban was carrying two beers in his hand. One of them was for somebody else, but now he didn't remember who. This time he answered truthfully:

'I haven't run into anyone. I haven't heard them either. The good thing about old buildings is you don't hear anything.'

'If I were you I'd find out right away who I'm going to be surrounded by for the rest of my days.'

A couple came over to say goodbye. Esteban took advantage of the opportunity to break free from Clemente. Their conversation was starting to bother him. He decided to avoid him the rest of the night. He was a negative guy whose paranoia was usually contagious.

Another thing Esteban made it a point to show his friends was the answering machine. A relic that he found amusing.

He liked showing people something that had gone obsolete. He enjoyed thinking back to the time when answering machines were in vogue, all those voices being recorded, being heard inside lonely houses. Ghosts talking to ghosts.

The last guest left at six in the morning. Esteban managed to get his shoes off and collapsed beside Adela, who was in a deep sleep. He put his arm around her and gave in to the warmth emanating from her body, to the fog of alcohol, to sleep.

The buzzer rang at seven a.m. Esteban heard it between dreams, incapable of getting up. Adela shook him awake.

'He's asking for you.'

With his eyelids still shut, Esteban asked, 'Who?'

'Señor Ligotti.'

His eyes opened in surprise.

'What does he want? Tell him I'm sleeping.'

Adela sat down on the bed.

'I already told him. But he insists on seeing you. He says the two of you agreed on it.'

'We agreed?'

'That you would see each other. Go talk to him. It gives me the creeps thinking of him out there waiting.'

Esteban got up reluctantly and put on his shoes. He didn't splash water on his face nor comb his hair, hoping that his appearance would discourage the unwelcome visitor.

He opened the apartment door. Señor Ligotti was waiting in the hallway, resting on his walking stick.

'It's about time.'

Although he was half asleep, Esteban recognized the anomaly.

'How did you get in the building?'

'A neighbor was going out. Everyone here knows me.'

'I haven't seen anyone in days . . .'

Señor Ligotti came closer.

'Aren't you going to invite me in?'

Esteban hesitated. The old man's visit was ill-timed, but he couldn't be rude to him. After all, he had helped him to buy the place. He stepped to one side and with a wave of his hand invited him to enter.

'Of course, come in.'

He added in an ironic tone:

'Make yourself at home.'

The visit was hell. Señor Ligotti chattered indefatigably and seemed to have no intention of leaving quickly. Esteban's head ached from the hammering of his hangover. He could hardly follow the old man's chit-chat, which went from one pointless topic to another. Amid his discomfort, he realized something: he had idealized him. When he met him, he struck him as a humanist, a philanthropist, a dying breed that he'd had the luck to run across. Now he saw him clearly: he was arrogant, maniacal, presumptuous. Why the hell had he come? And so early. That's how loners were: they had no sense of other people's time. They required as much attention as children. On top of everything, Adela had fled, pretending she had to go visit her mother, leaving him at the mercy of his 'guest'.

Esteban dozed off at times. Every time he opened his eyes he found that Señor Ligotti was still going on with his endless monologue. He caught some phrases that troubled him, questions the old man asked without waiting for a response: *'How's the new book going? What's it about? I suppose you haven't got very far. Something will have to be done so that you make progress, so that you swing, so that you ring . . .'*

In the end he fell asleep. When he awoke, shaken again by Adela, it was already night. When had Ligotti left? He thought the visit had been a bad dream, a nightmare brought on by his hangover. But on the living room table he saw the ring with the National University logo.

Adela picked it up and said sarcastically:
'Now your *friend* has an excuse to come back.'

Señor Ligotti turned into a problem. He would show up at any day and time, with an attitude that bordered on demanding. Besides being annoyed, Esteban was worried: this wasn't a case of indiscretion but of obsession. The old man returned on the day following his first visit. Esteban gave him back the ring, thinking that would keep him away for a while, but he kept coming back. Sometimes he rang the buzzer outside the building, other times directly at the apartment door. What was most disturbing was his way of ringing, insistently, as if he were there to deliver an urgent package.

Esteban began to avoid him. If Señor Ligotti came to the door, he would open it saying he had an important appointment and, after apologizing, would set off down the street at a brisk pace. He would also pretend there was no one home until the old man finally left. One time when he was coming back from the store, he saw him at a distance, standing at the building's front door. He immediately turned around, hopped in a taxi, and went to see a movie. At first this game of cat and mouse seemed funny. Adela spent most of her time at her mother's; dodging the old man became a source of entertainment for Esteban. A kind of challenge: to see who wore out first. The old man won't hold out longer than me, he told himself. Several days passed in this way, until the episode with the answering machine.

It was a gray afternoon, with clouds that presaged rain. Esteban was in his study reading Clemente's new novel. He was curious to find out if it was as bad as the previous ones. The intercom buzzer sounded. He peeked through the kitchen window, which looked out onto the street. It was polarized glass, which allowed him to see without being seen. He saw it was Señor Ligotti and returned to his chair. After a few minutes, the buzzer stopped ringing. Esteban could go back to concentrating on his reading. Thunder sounded, a downpour started to fall.

Something distracted him from the book. A strange feeling: he wasn't alone. There was a presence, not within the house, but outside. Through the kitchen window he saw a disconcerting image: Señor Ligotti was still outside, standing in the rain, staring at the building. The old man took a cell phone out of his bag and dialed a number.

The apartment's telephone rang.

Esteban let it ring. He felt the muscles in his body twitch, as if they were shrinking. The answering machine switched on. Señor Ligotti's irritated voice boomed:

'I know you're there. Open up.'

He tried to recall: had he given him his number?

'You must let me in. Fulfill your part of the bargain.'

He had an absurd, unsettling thought: the old man could see him, his gaze penetrated the polarized glass. He didn't dare to move, like a cockroach surprised when a light is turned on.

Señor Ligotti didn't say anything more. He just stood there with the phone to his ear, getting soaked. The rain could be heard outside, and through the answering machine as well. It was an unreal sound effect, the echo of a nightmare. The machine's tape reached the end and the recording cut off, breaking the spell. Esteban reacted by going to his room. He got in bed, hiding under the covers like he did as a child.

Adela suggested they go on vacation. 'You're really tense,' she told him, 'it would do you good to get out of the city.' The next morning they got in the car and took the highway. When the first cows appeared, Esteban started to feel better. They stayed at a resort with thermal baths. They were sunny days, with a lot of reading. Clemente's novel was rubbish, and that helped to improve his state of mind. It had too many legalistic details that dragged down the plot. A lot of knowledge about the judicial system, not much of a story.

Adela and Esteban devoted themselves to the vacation. They swam. They stuffed themselves with food. They made love slowly so they wouldn't hurt the baby.

A week later, Esteban felt back to normal. He thought about his behavior the past few days, the irrational fear that the old man had aroused in him. Now he knew what to do. He would confront him. He would put a stop to the situation. If necessary, he would shout the truth in his face. He was nothing more than a senile old coot, washed-up, pathetic. On the way home his confidence grew. The end of the problem was nearing, the solution was in his hands.

He never imagined what would be waiting for him at home.

He opened the apartment door. Señor Ligotti was inside, clinking his rings against a steaming cup of coffee.

After the initial shock came the anger. Adela looked at Esteban, blurted out a *Get him out of here, I never want to see him here again*, and locked herself in the bedroom. Señor Ligotti sipped his coffee with a carefree air, as if his being there were the most natural thing in the world, which only infuriated Esteban more. He stood in front of him, containing his desire to hit him.

'This time you've gone too far. How did you get in? The neighbors helped you with that too?'

The old man shook his head no. Then he smiled, amused.

'I have a set of keys. And since you haven't lived up to your part of the bargain, I felt obliged to use them.'

'What bargain?'

'We agreed that I would visit you. It was the pact we made before signing the contract.'

'You're crazy. Don't you get it? Nobody wants you here. Get lost or I'll call the police.'

'That's no way to treat a guest.'

Señor Ligotti stood up, but instead of going to the door he headed towards the kitchen, where he poured himself another cup of the coffee he had made.

Esteban went after him, furious.

'Get out of here! I'll have you thrown in jail, I swear it!'

The old man leaned his hip against the kitchen sink; he took a sip of his drink while he looked at him defiantly.

Esteban turned around, went to the telephone and dialed the emergency number. 'Home invasion,' he said, raising his voice so that the elderly man would hear him.

He went back to the kitchen. Señor Ligotti gave a cackling laugh.

'Home invasion? Seriously? That's the problem with not writing. Writing is like a muscle, and when it's not used, the language atrophies. I urge you to get back to your keyboard. In fact, it would do you good to write longhand: the sentences flow better that way.'

His speech was interrupted by the doorbell. The police had arrived quickly.

Esteban gave the old man a cruel look.

'You won't be laughing about this.'

He went to open the door. He led the officers to the kitchen. There was nobody inside, only the steaming cup. They searched the rest of the house: nothing.

Señor Ligotti had vanished. Just like a ghost.

The next person to ring was the locksmith. Esteban told him he wanted a new high-security lock. He also thought about changing the one on the building's front door, but first he had to talk to the neighbors. Where the hell were they hiding? He was overcome by a mixture of feelings. On the one hand, rage; on the other, embarrassment. He had made a fool of himself with the police. The officers looked at him with suspicion, no doubt they thought he was paranoid, a prankster even. Adela was no help. Instead of serving as a witness, she turned against him: it hadn't been a good idea to buy that apartment. I TOLD YOU SO. The police finally left without taking their statements.

The days that followed were even stranger. Esteban slept fitfully, awakened by nightmares in the middle of the night. On one occasion he opened his eyes amidst the darkness, overcome by a feeling of anxiety. It was raining. He lay there listening to the sound of the drops hitting the window panes. Suddenly he could make out a silhouette sitting in a chair at the foot of the bed. A flash of lightning lit up the room, allowing him to recognize Señor Ligotti. He realized that the sound he heard was produced by the old man's rings tapping the cup he held in his hands.

Si non oscillas, noli tintinnare.

He awoke with a stifled scream. It was morning. Adela was in the bathroom. The sound of the shower could be heard through the door.

He became increasingly certain that he was losing his mind. That dream had been too real; he was starting to have a hard time telling whether he was awake or asleep. Things got worse a few days later, when he found Señor Ligotti's ring on the bureau. The birds on the National University logo spreading their wings like a menace. Adela tried to calm him down: he probably left it the day he let himself in with his keys and you hadn't noticed it. Amid all his confusion, Esteban had one certainty: he couldn't count on his wife. She was only thinking about the baby, she rejected any additional worries. He opted not to tell her anything for now. He kept silent about each new discovery, each message – he was sure that's what they were – that the old man left him: a visiting card (he gave it to you when you met him, don't be paranoid, Adela would have said), a little glass bell that he had never seen in the house before, more rings . . .

Señor Ligotti was a demiurge, there was no other explanation. A demiurge or a demon, and the solution was to call a priest to exorcize the house. He had made up his mind to go to the neighborhood church and look into the possibility when he made another disturbing discovery.

He was trying to read in the living room, but couldn't concentrate. He felt a draft of cold air coming from the floor. Esteban crouched down and approached the fireplace on all fours. The frozen air hit him in the face. He stretched out his hand to touch the back and it gave way, revealing an opening behind it. The fireplace had a metal plate the same color as the wall, an effective camouflage. Esteban went through the hole. It proved to be a passage, full of leaves and branches, which led to the building's side courtyard. There was another removable plate there through which one could go outside.

Señor Ligotti was not a phantom. He was something worse: a dangerous madman.

A mason took care of covering the hole in the fireplace. He laid bricks and mortar and afterwards added a coat of paint. Meanwhile, Esteban went over the house inch by inch in search of more passages. He checked closets, the flooring, under the sink. Also doors and windows: he wanted to close off any possibility whatsoever of intrusion. Adela waited patiently while he did all this and then said they needed to talk. She didn't want to fight or argue, she told him. Things had gotten out of control. She wanted to get out of there as soon as possible . . .

They were interrupted by a sound coming from the door. With a wave of his hand, Esteban asked his wife to wait. He went to the door armed with a kitchen knife. On the floor he saw an envelope. He bent down to pick it up and opened it with trembling hands.

It was an eviction notice.

Esteban had a moment of clarity. One where the events of

the past few days fit perfectly, where his stupidity and laziness played a central role. In one of the desk drawers he found the contract he had signed with Señor Ligotti. He tried to read it, but he couldn't: the letters became blurry, shaky. He scanned it, emailed it to Clemente and asked him to review it as soon as possible. 'You're the expert on legal stuff,' he told him in the message.

The telephone rang a few minutes later. His friend's first words puzzled him even more:

'You sent the wrong document.'

'What?'

'The purchase contract you sent me is incomplete and therefore invalid. The last sheet is a different contract, to publish a book.'

Esteban took the document he had scanned: it was the right one, there was no question. In the first paragraph he read: 'Ligotti Industries declares that . . .' He felt nauseous, on the verge of fainting.

'It's the one I signed.'

'The old man screwed you. For legal purposes, you didn't get an apartment: you promised to write a novel within a year.'

'He's very clever. He got me to sign without my noticing the trick . . .'

Esteban summarized the recent events for his friend.

'What am I going to do? I'm ruined.'

Clemente tried to calm him:

'I'll investigate Ligotti with my court contacts. I'm sure we'll find something shady in his past, something that might help you. Meanwhile, don't leave your apartment or you'll lose it.'

When he hung up, Adela already had her suitcase ready. She was going to her mother's house. Esteban agreed: it was the best thing to do. For her to be safe while he sorted out the serious mistake he had made. He would barricade himself in the apartment. It was his home. He had poured all the money he had into it.

To take it away from him, they would have to kill him.

When he was young, Esteban experienced something similar. His parents spent years saving with the goal of buying a house. After great sacrifices they collected enough for the down payment. The family moved from the small apartment where they were living to a two-story house with a yard and garage. To celebrate, they invited relatives and friends over for a meal: everyone hugged them, congratulating them on their new lifestyle. Esteban met the neighbor kids his own age, soon he was playing football and hide-and-seek with them.

That phase didn't last. His parents were smothered by the expenses; they stopped making the monthly payments on the house, they ended up losing it. Esteban never forgot the day they moved out: the neighbors looking out their doors and windows with pitying faces, the sense of profound shame at the public exhibition, the defeat in his father's tired expression, his mother's tears, his older brothers' silence.

Now history was being repeated. The family curse that condemned them to be eternal renters. However, there was a difference: with his parents it had been financial miscalculation. By contrast, he had let himself be tricked like a child. And it wasn't just the apartment that was at stake.

He could lose Adela. He could lose his sanity.

He sat on the living room sofa for hours, watching the sealed-up hole in the fireplace as if he expected to see Señor Ligotti come out of it, until night fell. He put his thoughts aside, got up, and flipped the light switch.

Nothing happened.

He went through the house pressing the other switches, with the same result. Just what he needed: the power had gone out. He didn't have a flashlight, nor candles. The time had come to ask the neighbors for a favor. Maybe he could even get some information out of them about Señor Ligotti.

He went out into the hall. It was lit by a milk-white bulb, the outage had occurred only in his apartment. He knocked on the door next to his and realized it was partway open. He didn't want to be taken for an intruder, so he said loudly:

'Hello . . .'

There was no response. He knocked again, this time louder, and then added:

'I'm your neighbor, my power's out.'

When no one answered, he pushed the door a little and stuck his head in. The hall light allowed him to see that the apartment was empty. It smelled damp, musty. The floor was bulging, rotten. It was obvious it had been abandoned for a long time.

He headed for the next apartment. Its door was also ajar; he knocked and waited several seconds, then opened it slowly, as if he wanted to delay the moment of revelation.

There was nothing inside except for a forgotten paint can.

Was it a coincidence? There was only one more apartment, at the end of the hall. If he found it empty he would go up to the next floor and the next, until he found someone.

He walked, listening to the amplified echo of his steps. He felt like the ghost of a lonely castle. A lost soul in eternal search of companionship.

The door was closed. He put his ear against it: silence. Nothing seemed to be moving inside. He put his hand on the knob; it wasn't locked, so he was able to turn it, producing the grinding sound made by rusty objects. He was going to enter, but he was stopped by the ringing of a telephone behind him. He stood frozen for a few seconds until he realized it was his. He ran to his apartment and answered it, panting.

He heard Clemente's voice.

'Get out of there right now!'

Esteban caught his breath and asked:

'What are you saying? Why?'

'I found out some things about Ligotti. Get your things and get out! There's no time for explanations.'

Esteban had left his apartment door open. He saw that the hall light was going out. Then he heard someone unlocking the front door of the building.

Before the line went dead, Clemente managed to say:

'Ligotti owns the whole building.'

That day in his childhood when Esteban and his family moved from the house they had lost to a tiny apartment, something strange happened. He woke up thirsty in the middle of the night, he felt feverish, claustrophobic. His older brothers snored in their bunks, resigned to the overcrowding. He went to the kitchen for a glass of water. He wanted a little air too, some space.

A glow coming from the living room caught his attention. The TV was on. The screen showed colored bars indicating the channel was off-air. Esteban had always found them enigmatic: a signal, the key to an encoded message. He saw his father's silhouette outlined against the light. He had fallen asleep in the chair. He went up to him to wake him; he was surprised to discover his eyes open, fixed on the screen.

'What are you doing, Daddy?'

His father didn't notice his presence. Esteban was going to speak to him again but something stopped him. He didn't know then; but now, as he held the telephone in his hand, as he listened to the emptiness of the line that had gone dead, taking Clemente's voice along with it, he understood what it had been.

Señor Ligotti's figure appeared in the doorway. He recognized him despite the darkness: in one hand he gripped his walking stick.

He hadn't said anything more to his father because his empty gaze contained a warning. Something sinister was living inside him and if he broke the trance it would emerge with all its power. The bars on the TV kept it at bay. It was better to leave it like that.

Underneath people's skin there were monsters, like the one he now had to face.

Energized by the whiplash of adrenaline, Esteban looked around for things he could use to hurt his attacker. The darkness only let him discern the largest objects: a chair, a dresser, a plant, nothing he could use as a weapon. He weighed his chances. Señor Ligotti was crazy, but he was an old man. It would be easy to subdue him. Various images passed through his head: he would shove him down, straddle him, give him some humiliating slaps. He wanted to see him break, hear him cry. The rage built up in recent days overflowed. Opening his mouth, Esteban let out a sharp, primitive, animal cry and sprang at his rival.

He failed to knock him down.

Señor Ligotti easily sidestepped his attack, then struck his cane across his face, breaking his nose. Esteban fell to the floor, bleeding profusely. The old man bent down, grabbed him by one foot and began to drag him down the hallway.

While he was being hauled like a sack, Esteban wondered: where did the old man get such strength? He saw a flash of lightning and heard the rain start to come down. Where was he taking him? He tried to escape, but his strength failed him. The darkness became thicker, he lost consciousness.

The cold rain woke him. The world had gone upside down, the buildings hung from an asphalt sky. It took him a moment to realize that he was upside down on the roof of the building, that his body was hanging over the edge. He looked towards his feet and saw that Señor Ligotti was holding him by one leg. How had he gotten him all the way up there?

The old man started to swing him. Slowly, from left to right, moving his body like a pendulum.

Overcoming his fear, Esteban sought answers:

'Why are you doing this to me? What do you want? Answer me!'

A lightning flash illuminated the old man's face. In that final moment, Esteban understood. Señor Ligotti looked at him with a mixture of curiosity and impatience, the same way a human observes the slow movements of a mollusk. He wasn't a madman: he was a higher being. A god who was toying with him, like a boy playing with ants.

The old man's voice rose above the sound of the wind and rain:

'Si non oscillas, noli tintinnare.'

Esteban felt him let go, the vertigo of the fall, the abyss sucking him towards a certain death. He closed his eyes and hugged himself, anticipating the position of his body in its shroud.

But he didn't fall. Señor Ligotti grabbed his leg again, then dragged his body over the edge of the terrace and set him down safely on the roof. Esteban lay there curled up in a ball, trembling and crying like a newborn baby. The old man leaned over him. He brushed the wet hair back from his face and pushed it behind his ears. Then he kissed him on the forehead.

Esteban closed his eyes, fearing the real denouement: his rival's hands strangling him or disemboweling him with a knife.

He opened them seconds later. Señor Ligotti had disappeared.

When the police visited him in the hospital, where he was recovering from an unavoidable rhinoplasty, Esteban decided not to press charges against Señor Ligotti. He was terrified to face him again, to have a confrontation with him. He stated that, because of the darkness, he hadn't been able to see his attacker's face; that he had no enemies nor the slightest idea of who had been responsible for the assault.

While this was going on, Clemente took care of moving everything from the apartment in Calle de Berlín to Adela's mother's house. Esteban didn't want to set foot in that place again. He would await his child's imminent birth under the shelter of his mother-in-law's roof. Afterwards, calmly, he would seek a new home for his family.

The birth and the first month of infancy kept his mind busy. However, it wasn't long before he fell into a deep depression. He started therapy with a psychologist who, after hearing his horrifying story about Señor Ligotti, suggested he commit it to paper.

'You could try writing a novel. It would help you. Isn't that what you writers do all the time? Exorcize your traumas through literature . . .'

Esteban was reluctant at first but wound up taking his advice. After a slow, painful start, when he was on the verge of abandoning the project, he entered an inspired catharsis: the ideas flowed at a dizzying rhythm, the plot fit together with a coherency he had never before experienced. Four months later he finished the novel, which he entitled *Señor Ligotti*. He sent it to several publishers, certain that he had just written his best book.

The first offer didn't take long to arrive. To his delight, it came from Grau Press. The novel, retitled by some genius in the marketing department as *Sinister Stalking*, was an immediate success. His bank account grew just as quickly, and he was able to get a modest apartment on the outskirts of the city. This time he hired a lawyer to handle the contract.

Fortune smiled on him. But Esteban was no longer naive, he couldn't be after recent events.

Everything had a price. It was just a matter of waiting for the bill collector to show up.

★

His son turned two. During all this time, Esteban didn't write anything. *Sinister Stalking* kept being reprinted; the royalties it generated were enough for them to live well and he preferred to devote himself to his family. He didn't miss creative work and even stayed away from public events. He started to think of retiring, of the possibility of remaining connected to literature through teaching. A couple of universities showed interest in hiring him. Maybe, he sometimes mused in the dead of night when suffering from insomnia, he had written all he had to write.

There was also another possibility: that he was paralyzed by the fear of not being able to beat *Sinister Stalking*'s success.

As if divining his thoughts, the director of Grau Press called one morning to invite him to the office. 'We have to talk,' he said. Esteban accepted out of politeness: it was his publisher, he lived off them, he couldn't say no. He saw it as a courtesy visit.

As he checked in at the lobby, he was relieved not to see Ligotti Industries' name in the directory. He relaxed even more when he got off the elevator on the top floor and discovered that his old enemy's offices were for rent. Where had he gone? Had he died? Who cared. The truth was that he was glad to avoid him.

The director received him with forced enthusiasm. He was an executive who didn't know much about books; on the other hand, he mastered numbers and accounts to perfection. They made small talk for a long while. Esteban felt increasingly uncomfortable. He started to look for an excuse to get out of there.

Suddenly the director took his arm and led him down a hallway.

'Actually, it's the owner who wants to speak with you.'

Esteban was surprised. He had never dealt with him.

'And to what do I owe the honor?'

'He's worried because you haven't sent in anything new . . .'

They arrived in front of a huge wooden door. It was old, with elegant carvings. On the upper part, in the middle, a phrase was inscribed:

SI NON OSCILLAS, NOLI TINTINNARE

Esteban's back stiffened. His vision clouded and he felt the urge to vomit.

The director put his hand on the doorknob.

'. . . and when an author gets writer's block, he likes to help. He has certain methods for stimulating the imagination.'

The door opened, the director pushed him inside. Esteban was petrified, unable to open his eyes, until he heard a voice:

'Welcome. Sit down.'

It belonged to a young man. Esteban raised his eyelids. Behind the desk he saw a guy with blond hair, smooth-faced, with horn-rimmed glasses. He felt ridiculous. His paranoia had gotten the better of him again. The solution was obvious: Señor Ligotti knew this office; no doubt this was where he'd gotten the phrase from.

He approached the desk, still dizzy from the shock, and sat down.

'Sorry, I don't feel well.'

He closed his eyes again. The air in the office was thick, hot; Esteban felt he was suffocating.

With excessive familiarity, the owner asked him:

'Are you hungover?'

Then, changing the subject, he added:

'I have something for you . . .'

Esteban heard him open a drawer. Then he heard something that terrified him, a sound that confirmed what he already feared: that his nightmare was really just beginning.

' . . . it's the contract for a new book.'

Behind him, from some corner of the office, the sound continued to be heard.

The jingling of a hand loaded with rings.

Come to Me

'Long for him with all your soul,' the witch doctor had told her, and Laurinda had done just that. Months later, as she waited in the semi-darkness of her bedroom for Raúl to return, she considered the consequences of her actions for the first time. He might knock on the door at any moment, transformed into something unimaginable. There was no going back. And even if she could turn back time, she would do things the same way: she would take the flyer, would once again dial the number for the shaman who promised BONDS GUARANTEED FOR LIFE. THE MAN OF YOUR DREAMS WILL STAY BY YOUR SIDE FOREVER. When she saw it in the newspaper, Laurinda felt her prayers had been answered. For two years now she had been hopelessly in love with her office mate, Raúl, but he had always blown her off. No matter how often she approached his cubicle on some pretext or other, or schemed to bump into him at lunch, all she ever got was a cold greeting and noncommittal phrases. Her patience had run out; if somebody had a solution to offer her, even if it seemed crazy, she was ready to take it. Laurinda didn't hesitate. In exchange, her wishes came true, to the surprise of her family and friends. There was a period of immense happiness, a paradise where nothing but the two of them existed. But now she was about to learn the true price of her temerity.

That's what she thought, but she was wrong. What she would witness in a few seconds was only a preview, a *sample*.

She pricked up her ears in the darkness. She heard noises on the stairs. They weren't exactly footsteps. Not those of a normal man, full of life. It was a sound of earth moving, of something making its way along with roots and stones.

Before the noises stopped, Laurinda saw a mass of maggots crawling under her door.

How long does happiness last? Laurinda knew now that it was impossible to measure. It didn't matter whether it lasted seven days or seven years: once you lost it, it was like you'd never had it. It even turned against you: every memory, every instant recalled meant a torture that transformed the moments of pleasure into something blurred and unreal. Was that stroll along the shore of a lake one Sunday morning real? Had she dreamt it? Or was it a plan they had never gone through with? It didn't matter: it hurt unbearably. They never talked about having kids, she was sure of that. But that detail tormented her all the same. For Laurinda, that was the definition of happiness: what you experienced, or didn't experience, takes its toll sooner or later. Sometimes too soon.

That's what had happened to her.

A brief encounter with happiness. And then, the rest of her life.

In the wake of the accident, which happened six months after the wedding, Laurinda met with the witch doctor. She was devastated, but was still brave enough to confront him with his fraud. He had promised the bond would be forever, and now her husband was dead. Dead and buried. The shaman calmed her down. He got rid of the other customers who were waiting for him and fixed her a special tea for her nerves. He assured her that he was the best witch doctor she could have gone to. His power was so great that even an unforeseen circumstance of this magnitude wouldn't break his spell. All she had to do was go home. And wait.

'If you really love your husband,' he said, 'you'll accept him no matter what. *No matter how he comes back.*'

Laurinda obeyed. That same night, Raúl came home. He stood in the bedroom doorway, while the maggots falling from his body moved on the floor with the same clumsiness as him. Laurinda overcame her shock; she took his hand and led him to the shower. She bathed him, removed crusts of dirt and mud, dressed him in clean clothes. Even so, she had a hard time recognizing him: his face was only a skull with some remnants of rotted flesh, and he had the expression of someone asleep with his eyes open. After sitting him down in his favorite chair, Laurinda sat watching him until dawn. If this is the new Raúl, she told herself, I'd better get used to him quickly.

And she would have, but two days later she got a call from her brother-in-law.

'You can stop by whenever you want,' he said. 'Or if you'd rather, I can come by and give them to you.'

Laurinda didn't understand, but she felt a chill nonetheless. She thought maybe it was from the glass of milk she'd just poured from the refrigerator.

'What are you talking about?'

There was a silence on the other end while her brother-in-law tried to find the right words.

'Well, maybe you don't remember. You were really upset at the time, so I had to be the one to make the decision . . . I'm talking about the ashes.'

The glass slid through Laurinda's fingers and shattered on the floor.

'That's impossible,' she managed to stammer.

'Are you all right?' her brother-in-law asked with growing unease. 'We can talk about it some other time.'

'It's impossible,' Laurinda repeated, as she looked over at the chair where Raúl had sat the entire time since coming to the house.

At that moment, Raúl – or whoever it was – got up and headed towards her.

★

What had gone wrong? Laurinda replayed in her mind the ritual that the witch doctor had made her perform to attract the attention of the man she loved. After saying several prayers at an altar on which some locks of Raúl's hair rested, the shaman put the hair in a plastic bag and used a piece of tape to attach it to Laurinda's breast, near her heart. As he instructed her, she wore it for a month without taking it off even when bathing. Before going to bed, she repeated the words 'Come to me' until she fell asleep. She followed it all to the letter. Yet something had gone wrong, because now that she had this corpse in front of her, which seemed to have suddenly come to life and was now bringing its rotted face closer in an attempt to kiss her with its nonexistent lips, she realized it wasn't Raúl. Who was it then? She had to find out at once.

Laurinda fled her house. She left the door open in the hope that when she got back the abomination would be gone. She went to the witch doctor's shop. This time he made her wait while he tended to other customers. In the little sitting area adjoining the ritual room, Laurinda had time to study those faces. She saw the same expression on all of them: distress and blind faith in a magical solution. Probably, she thought, the same expression as mine.

When it was her turn, she explained to the shaman the extent of the problem.

'They cremated him. It can't be him.'

'Where did you get his hair?' the witch doctor asked, after a few seconds' thought.

'From the salon he always goes to. I know somebody who works there. Ángeles and I have been friends since we were kids.'

'You collected it, or you entrusted it to her?'

'I asked her to do me a favor. I didn't dare go to the salon at the same time as Raúl. It would have been so obvious.'

The shaman took a small cigar from his shirt pocket and lit

it. He waited until his mouthful of smoke had dispersed, then declared:

'Even though he was cremated, he can still come back. It'll just take longer. The bottom line is that your friend gave you the wrong hair. You have to talk to her. That's the only way we'll find out who's in your house now.'

The meeting was in a café near the salon. At first Ángeles acted evasively, but seeing her friend's growing desperation she decided to confess. There was no doubt in her mind that the loss of her husband was driving Laurinda to the brink of madness; however, she figured the best thing to do was tell her the truth and keep her distance from her for a while.

'I didn't think it was that important,' she said nervously. 'I've never believed in hocus pocus.'

'I trusted you.' Laurinda could hardly contain herself. 'Whose hair did you give me?'

'I don't know.'

'What do you mean, you don't know!' Laurinda exploded. 'There's a corpse living in my house and I have to get rid of it.'

Ángeles couldn't conceal her expression of shock. Laurinda was raving. She wanted to flee, but she was afraid Laurinda would follow her.

'The day Raúl came to the salon I was running late. It was my coworker who did his hair. When I got there, he was already gone. I grabbed a handful of hair out of the trash. That's what I gave you.'

Laurinda leaned over the table and spoke in low tones, as if suddenly afraid someone might overhear their conversation.

'Do you know if any of the salon's customers have died lately?'

'Yes – ' Ángeles' fear grew – 'Señor Gonzalo. He had a heart attack.'

Laurinda knew she wasn't asking the crucial question. Her

eyes filled with tears at the certainty that her problem was worse than she had imagined.

'There were multiple customers' hair mixed in that handful you gave me, right?'

'I'm afraid so. The ones from that day and the ones from the day before, since we hadn't taken the trash out yet.'

Laurinda put her hands to her face and began to cry.

When was the last time she saw Raúl? That too was blurry. She didn't remember whether she was awake when he left on that business trip and they'd said goodbye in the kitchen, or if it was the night before, as they fell asleep in each other's arms like usual. What she did know was that she got a call at the office at noon; the person on the other end informed her that her husband had been in a car accident and was in very serious condition. A stranger, was the first thing she thought when she got the news. What right does a complete stranger have to tell me a thing like that? Oddly enough, the fact that it was the cold words of some unknown person made her realize their real meaning: that her days of happiness were over. From a relative she would have expected comfort, the hackneyed 'Everything will be all right'. That stranger was the perfect messenger for marking a before and after in her personal story. The moment she hung up the phone Laurinda was aware her life would never be the same. Or, to be more precise, that it would go back to being exactly the same as before she got married. A life she had done everything possible to escape from, and which was now coming back to her like a curse.

She had been parked in front of her house for an hour, her hands gripping the steering wheel. Laurinda didn't dare to enter what, until that morning, had been home to her alone. The events of the past several months, but especially the words of the witch doctor, thronged in her head. After leaving Ángeles at the café, Laurinda went to the shaman and told him what she'd found out. He seemed to be fed up with her. His response was ruthless:

'The spell was cast with the hair of multiple men, there's nothing that can be done to undo it. People underestimate the power of spells and don't take the appropriate caution when performing them. You've made a big mistake, your destiny is to pay for it. As these people die, whenever it's their time – as happened with Señor Gonzalo – they'll come and find you. Maybe one of them will be Raúl, maybe not. How can you know if his hair was really among those locks salvaged from the trash? And if he shows up at your house one day, could you recognize him behind his fleshless face? You are going to see a series of monstrosities parade through your life with no other object than to profess their love to you.'

Their *eternal* love, thought Laurinda.

'Do you understand what I'm telling you?' the witch doctor concluded with a sneer.

Yes. Laurinda understood very well. She was condemned to collect dead suitors. Nevertheless, one of them could be Raúl. *Had* to be him. She had the rest of her life to wait for him.

She looked at her reflection in the rearview mirror. She wiped the mascara that was running down her cheeks, fixed her hair. Then she got out of the car and walked towards the house with firm steps.

Demoness

'The demon's target is not the possessed; it is us the observers.'
— William Peter Blatty

Late that night, amid the intense heat, the smell of urine and vomit, and his companions' prayers, there was a moment of calm in the kitchen. Then Ismael was able to collapse onto a chair and sleep. And he dreamed. He dreamed about a girl who was lost in the woods by daylight. The girl found a path and at the end of that path was a house with a smoking chimney. The girl knocked on the door, relieved, and the person who opened the door was herself. With the same red dress and the same blue eyes. 'Let me in,' she said to herself, 'I'm scared.' 'I can't let you in,' came the response from inside the house. 'Why not?' 'Because if I do, the story is over. The fact that I'm in here means the story has an ending, but you can't get to it without venturing into the forest at night first.' The girl went off, sad and resigned. 'Make sure you're able to get back here,' she yelled to herself from the doorway. 'What do you care?' she answered herself from the path. 'You're already safe.' 'You're wrong. If you don't come back, the story changes. And I change too.' The girl understood. She smiled maliciously from the path and waved goodbye. And she went off, relieved again. She knew that she wouldn't be back. That it wasn't the story of a little girl lost in the woods. It was the story of a haunted house.

★

I

Everyone's eyes settled on the fire. The wood crackled as it split, and a series of sparks flew past the edge of the hearth and fell onto the rug. Ismael stomped them out with his boots; then he grabbed the poker and shifted the logs around, rekindling the flames. He thought about what one of his professors had told him years earlier: 'That's what we psychiatrists do: put out fires. But we also start them up again.' How many forest fires had he started in his patients' minds before putting them out with tons of medications? He didn't know and he figured it didn't matter. 'It's better to burn out than fade away.' Who was it who said that? Some teen idol in a suicide note . . . He looked at his old high school friends, silent and pensive in the cabin's living room, wearing caps and woolen ponchos, taking constant sips from their glasses of tequila to ward off the icy night. They hadn't seen each other in twenty years and didn't have much to talk about. The Jesuits had brought them together in classrooms in the late '80s and now they were bringing them together again in the new century for an anniversary retreat in the mountains of Tapalpa. Their class was celebrating twenty years since they had graduated. Or retired, it was the same thing. From what he could tell at the welcome dinner, most of them now had too many kids, very little hair, and even less enthusiasm. And they were all only around forty. There would be a Mass early the next morning, so most of them had gone to bed. Only Alma, Alfredo, and Ignacio accepted the invitation to go on drinking in his cabin. They were all he needed. They had seen the same thing as he did years ago. They were part of the *episode*. And now it was almost time to start a new fire.

★

II

The tequila burned his throat, but in the rest of his body the cold was digging holes and crawling into the deepest one. Ignacio was shivering, though he was making a serious effort not to. He knew coming here hadn't been a good idea, and now he was being proved right. The Jesuits were friendly to him, but their looks were loaded with questions and reproaches. He had taken a sabbatical year from the faith, and now he had to decide whether to return to the priesthood or leave the Society. And the truth was that he still felt the same doubts. Coming here hurt for that very reason: because it was on the retreats the Jesuits used to organize in high school that he had discovered his calling and his love for the Society. While his friends were deciding to become doctors or lawyers, he saw himself following the revolutionary spirit of the Jesuits. Liberation theology had charmed him like a snake. He even came to imagine himself shot down as a martyr, defending the cause of the Central American guerillas. And now his faith was trying to rekindle itself, like the fire Ismael was poking at. The problem wasn't that he had stopped believing in God. He had stopped believing in himself ... He drank more tequila. The cold had made his penis hard, an erection concealed in the folds of his poncho. It happened whenever he was cold. He looked at Alma sitting on the wicker chair beside him, lost in her thoughts just like him. Her poncho hid her pointy breasts. But Ignacio knew very well what she had underneath. He had seen and touched. A memory now transformed into a recurring dream. He longed to put his arms around that body once more and devour it like a Communion wafer. He took another sip of tequila. The fire crackled in the fireplace but did nothing to warm his bones.

★

III

We are increasingly isolated tribes, Alfredo thought. Once we were nomads; now we've formed new settlements, seeking refuge in the family to flee from ourselves. He thought about breaking the silence with those words but didn't dare to. The anthropologist analyzing the evolution of species. He laughed to himself, but he knew it was silly to include himself in that scheme. How many ex-classmates had gathered that weekend for the retreat? Seventy? Eighty? And among them there was only a single species: homo-*matrimonius*. Ah, and homo-*divorciadus*, if he took himself into account. But an individual didn't make a species. He was an anomaly. So was Ignacio, but he didn't count. Wasn't he supposed to be married to God? The Jesuits were very clever because they didn't deny themselves a single pleasure: they smoked, drank, ate, and fucked like everybody else. And quite right too. For every priest who loved a woman, thought Alfredo, that's another kid safe … A single species, not at all appealing as something to analyze. That was the problem with class reunions: they didn't involve a living culture but archeological remains. What will future generations think when they dig up our bones? What will their analysis show? Fingers atrophied by remote controls, spinal columns overcome by bulging bellies, skulls eaten up by alopecia. The ancient Egyptians were buried with scarab amulets to protect them from the judgment of Osiris. The Aztecs with a green stone in their mouth that symbolized the heart. They'll bury us with our laptops and a network card so we can get online in the great beyond … Instinctively, Alfredo took out his phone and found for the umpteenth time that there was no signal. He needed to connect with someone from the city, someone outside. Send a message and get a response that would place him in the civilized world. The intangible world of modern communications. He thought about the wisdom of indige-nous peoples who made smoke signals and smiled again. That night he'd be capable of setting his car on fire if it meant being able to send a message to someone he knew.

IV

The silence didn't make her uncomfortable: in drama school she had done many exercises without speaking; what was missing from this unwelcoming room was movement. Alma saw the animal skulls and skins adorning the walls and thought that there were too many dead things in that cabin. Then she thought about suggesting a game of charades, that would be a good way to get the blood moving and break the block of ice that had formed among them despite the fireplace. At dinner, they had all been animated and talkative, but for some reason now they were all sunken in their own thoughts . . . Charades wasn't a good idea, too childish; maybe if she stood up and did a mime routine? Why was it so quiet? Only the fire and the shadow puppets it projected on the walls. At the banquet earlier they'd been distracted by the novelty and the effort of recognizing names and faces. But now the four of them were confronted with an abyss: the passage of twenty years. A void filled with questions, but no answers. That's why she accepted Ismael's invitation for a last drink: she preferred to face the nostalgia together instead of doing it in the loneliness of her own cabin. Would Ignacio remember the night they made out at one of the high school retreats? It had happened near where they were now, at the old Jesuit house in Tapalpa. Late that night, Ignacio was totally wasted; she, on the other hand, was horny enough to be willing to lose her virginity on the rough rocks they were lying on, listening to The Cure's 'A Forest' coming from a nearby campfire, a perfect soundtrack for the moment. Everything seemed exciting and mysterious to her, like the woods around them. They ran off with some of their friends while the Jesuits were sleeping. They went into the mountains to make a campfire and pass around a bottle of *charanda*. Ignacio couldn't get it up, so she unzipped his fly and started to blow him. She'd never had a cock in her mouth, and at first it was an unpleasant sensation: it was flaccid and tasted like urine, but as it began to get hard and she felt the erect member between her lips, she sucked it harder and with greater pleasure, as she felt her own crotch getting wet. She didn't stop sucking until Ignacio came, and then the epiphany occurred: that unprecedented explosion of semen running down her throat and dripping from her lips, hot and sticky on her chin and on her neck; there was so much of it that it trickled down to her tits, and it kept coming. What she experienced was intense, and she yielded to the urge to smear it all over her body: she wiped it on her nipples and her belly, on her buttocks and her thighs. Seconds later she was lying on her back, looking up at the Moon, feeling every pore of her skin pulsing, imagining what it would be like to bathe in a tub filled with semen . . .

Alma realized Ignacio was watching her and she blushed. It was like he had heard her thoughts. That's why silence isn't good, she told herself, because people can get into your head. She glanced at Ismael by the fireplace; he looked like he was about to say something and she felt relieved. In the end he was like every psychiatrist: they boast of being good listeners, but in reality they never shut up. If they did, they'd go crazy. Just like their patients.

V

He opened his mouth, but the words didn't come out at first. Ismael feigned a yawn to cover up his hesitation. Then he moved a couple of steps to take up a position in the middle of the room and addressed himself to his old classmates more decisively.

'On nights like this people usually tell scary stories.' He paused to make sure they were all listening and went on: 'We have the perfect setting: the dark of night, the woods, and a fire. But it's too . . . obvious, don't you think?'

'Telling stories around a fire is the oldest entertainment in the world.' Alfredo sat up in his chair, suddenly animated. 'It's in our blood. What's wrong with it?'

'The only thing wrong is that we don't have a storyteller.' Alma lifted her legs onto the chair and covered them with her poncho. 'I prefer a well-told story over any stupid game; if you pull out the dominoes, I'm going back to my cabin.'

'Hell, why do we need a writer when we have a professional actress?' Ignacio suddenly seemed to come to life. He went on talking as he made theatrical gestures. 'Act something for us, Alma; the fire is the backdrop and we're the audience.'

'We can do something even better,' Ismael spoke again. 'Writers are no good at telling stories aloud, that's why they write them down. But we're not going to start reading here, or acting – ' he made a gesture toward Alma – 'and scary stories around a fire, I repeat, are really cliché. I suggest something more original: each of us tells about a trauma from adolescence. Something that really happened to you and that you had a hard time getting over, or maybe still haven't gotten over. And in exchange for that honesty, there will be no judgments, no indiscretions. What we say here stays here.'

'You're going to psychoanalyze us?' Alfredo cut in. 'That's pretty cliché too . . .'

'Not at all. I really believe in traumas as engines of true stories. The best writers do nothing more than recount their traumas as if they were other people's. They're contagion artists.'

'Hmm, I don't know . . .' Alma hesitated a few seconds. 'It'd be something really private, wouldn't it?'

'It could work,' said Ignacio. 'If all of us really open up. Confessionals serve their purpose, believe it or not.'

'That's the key – ' Ismael sat down on the empty chair, his back to the fire – 'truthfulness. Nowadays even my patients come to my office to lie to themselves.' He picked up his glass of tequila from the table and went on: 'And since it was my suggestion, I have no choice: I'll go first.'

VI

I had several techniques for masturbating back then; some I came up with, others were shared by cousins or friends, but I'll focus on one in particular. Now that I think about it, it was pretty strange – maybe they all are: there was one that involved egg whites, another with a piece of ham – but this one definitely verged on sinister because it tried to replace a female body. It consisted of, literally, fornicating with a pillow. And cumming in it, of course. After all the horizontal bustle, it had to be cleaned, with the disgust which that entailed. For some reason that I connect with my Catholic upbringing, I always felt a repugnance towards my own semen, towards the fact of *erasing* the evidence of my *offense*. There was some guilt, but above all disgust. I remember that no matter how much I washed them, the pillows kept accumulating dark stains inside the pillowcases. One time my mother noticed them, puzzled, but connected them with her sister, who had been recovering at our house recently after plastic surgery on her face. My aunt had rested her head, covered in bloody bandages and tubes, in the guest room, and that prevented a more discerning analysis on my mother's part. Inevitably, my frenzied masturbation wound up leading me to the church confessional. When it was my turn to kneel before the priest, I told him, in the lowest tones possible and constantly fearing that those behind me would hear: 'Father, I confess that I've committed *impure* acts with my body.' I don't know where I got that phrase from, but what I do remember clearly is that the priest – it was always the same one – got very nervous hearing my confession, pale and sweaty even. But what I really want to tell you about is the time I was on holiday in Mexico City, at my cousins' house. One afternoon when everyone else had gone out and I was alone in the house, I carried a pillow into my aunt and uncle's room to relieve my horniness. The bed was really big; maybe that's why I was drawn to that room. When I'd finished, I lay there sprawled out, completely naked and exhausted. I was on the verge of falling asleep, but I heard the phone in the next room start ringing. I got up, put on my boxers, and opened the door to go answer it. Then I realized my uncle was coming up the stairs to his room. I immediately closed the door, locked it, and hurried to get dressed. I was just pulling up my pants when I heard my uncle struggling with the lock. I walked toward the door while he asked who was in there. I told him it was me and to wait because I was getting ready to take a bath. I finished getting dressed, but while I was buttoning my shirt – it was a polo – he used his key to enter. Obviously it was all really suspicious: there was a bath in the guest bedroom, there was no reason for me to be locked in there. Before he got to where I was – there was a little corridor leading to the bed – I managed to throw the pillow onto the other side of the bed. I made up a story about there being no hot water in the other bathroom. We went to check and turned on the taps. Hot water came out, of course, but my uncle just said, 'How weird,' and didn't ask any more questions. I suppose he was reassured when he found I wasn't locked up with his daughter, something I'd tried unsuccessfully one time, by the way, but that's another story. I don't remember how I managed to get the pillow back later, but for quite a while afterwards an unpleasant sensation settled in my stomach, something I carried around with me constantly, as

if there were a presence inside me, clawing at me every time I
thought about what happened. I hadn't been caught with my
hand in the cookie jar – on the pillow, I should say – but I felt
a deep shame. And, above all, I shuddered at the thought of
what would have happened if the phone hadn't rung at that
exact moment. That saving phone call. For me it was like
something out of a horror film.

VII

Ismael took the tequila bottle from the table and refilled his
glass. Now that he'd stopped gesturing and moving his hands,
the cold was returning to his body. Only his back was still
warm from the heat generated by the fireplace behind him.
It was unsettling, becoming aware of that part of his body
while losing the feeling in his face, arms, and legs; like he was
turning into the Back Man. He remembered a story he'd read
as a child: a man with no arms or legs who drags himself up
a staircase on his back. When he's almost to the top, he slides
back down to the ground. The man tries again, with the same
result, thirty times. But he doesn't give up: he repeats his cat-
erpillar or earthworm movements again and again, climbing
the steps pathetically like a kind of Sisyphus of the disabled.
When he finally manages to reach the next floor, his back
covered in bruises, he realizes he forgot why he wanted to
get up there. The place is completely empty, there's nothing
there to remind him of what he was after. All he sees are the
bare walls and the smooth floor. There are no windows or
scenery. There's only him, the Back Man, filling that unin-
habited room with his presence. At that moment, the Back
Man has an epiphany and realizes: he is the story's *raison d'être*.
And then he goes back down the stairs again.

A doubt came over Ismael: was it really something he'd
read as a child, or a dream? He thought: sometimes we attrib-

ute to someone else what we've created, and vice versa. It didn't matter: the best stories have a way of making us forget the name of the author but never the plot; those are the ones that return to us in the form of dreams. As such, they could have been written by anyone.

Ismael noticed that silence had taken over the room once more and hurried to say something:

'See? It's like jumping into an ice-cold pool: you have to do it quickly and without thinking, otherwise you'll never work up the nerve.'

'Curious: the pillow as a metaphor for woman.' Ignacio rubbed his hands together for warmth. 'Has that changed in your adult life?'

'We said no psychoanalysis. You'll just have to sleep on it. No pun intended ... And now that I've gone, Ignacio, it's your turn ...'

VIII

There used to be an urban legend that said if someone got really drunk, they just had to put a handful of ice cubes on their balls to sober up. We tried this 'remedy' on a number of occasions, and I honestly don't remember if it worked, probably because the ones trying to revive the sloshed guy were as drunk as he was. In hindsight it strikes me instead as a method of agreed-upon torture, since what I do clearly remember is that the drunk person would frown and mumble curses, obviously uncomfortable. More than once we even pulled down someone's pants by force if he wasn't sufficiently knocked out by the alcohol. In any case, it was a lot of fun. Until it happened to you. Over time, we did it to everyone in our circle of friends, which makes me think that the whole ice thing became a kind of rite. When it happened to me, I stopped going to parties for a long time. I even considered changing schools. You probably think I'm exaggerating, but hear me out. There were girls at the party on that occasion, which was unusual in our group. Not too many, three or four, but enough to make me anxious. I liked one of them a lot; I had tried to approach her at school, but now that I had her in front of me all I could think to do was drink faster. At some point that night I wound up passed out on a chair after downing several muppets back to back. You know, the drink that came in a tequila shotglass and someone would make you drink in a single gulp, finishing it off with a vigorous shake of your head. One of many stupid teenage rituals. Since there were women there, they carried me to the bathroom to 'revive' me in private, pretending to them that they were going to make me throw up. They sat me on the toilet, pulled down my pants, and right when they put the ice on me I got an erection. Don't ask me why, cold has always had that effect on me. Anyway, they immediately removed the ice cubes and my cock went limp again. Then, maliciously, they all took turns looking. They had discovered a variation in the routine and they weren't going to miss the chance to take advantage of it. They started to rub my balls with the ice cubes. The erection returned, along with a series of stifled groans that came from the depths of my consciousness. They went on masturbating me, laughing, until I ejaculated all over my stomach. One of them told me all this days later. That's how I'm able to reconstruct the facts in such detail. The only thing I witnessed was the final part. I wish I hadn't, but the orgasm made me lucid enough for a few moments to realize the most horrifying part. The girls had been watching the whole thing through the half-open door. Their faces showed pity and compassion, but above all curiosity. I knew it at once: from then on, for them I would be the Jerked-Off Boy. No first or last name. A story to tell in the school hallways. An anecdote to spread by word of mouth. A fucking urban legend.

★

IX

This time there wasn't a prolonged silence. Ignacio raised his shotglass and, with a broad smile on his face, said:

'Cheers! To our most famous ex-classmate!'

They all laughed and raised their drinks to toast. Oddly enough, the mood had lightened: they were drunk and expectantly awaiting those little acts of catharsis that Ismael had set in motion.

'I heard that story in school.' Alma's eyes shone in the twilight, excited. 'But I didn't know it was about you. I swear.'

Alfonso put his hand in his inner coat pocket, pulled out a cigar, and put it in his mouth without lighting it.

'Don't take away his fifteen minutes of fame.'

'Get out your notebooks, I still have time for autographs.'

'We said we wouldn't dig around in any of the stories – ' Ismael had gotten up to rekindle the fire – 'but it would be interesting to delve into teenage masturbation rituals. They're common in many cultures; Alfonso could tell us about that . . .'

'He's not the only expert.' Ignacio snatched Alfonso's cigar away from him and went on, parodying the solemn tones of an intellectual, 'Ancient peoples connected masturbation with religion: the Egyptians believed Osiris created the world by jerking off; the Greeks attributed this great pastime to Hermes, the messenger of the gods; the Hindus thought that Shiva invented war after being jerked off by the goddess Agni; and what about Krishna, the god of self-contemplation and true mascot of the jerkoffs.'

'Brilliant,' Alfonso started clapping. 'An A+ for you, young man.'

'It's no biggie.' Ignacio handed the cigar back. 'You're not the only one who reads *National Geographic*.'

'You went at it more from the theological side than

anthropological,' Ismael broke in, 'but you made me think of something: the Catholic Church is one of the few religions that explicitly prohibit masturbation. Maybe that's why the stories we're telling are so full of testosterone and semen.'

'It all stems from a misunderstanding – ' Ignacio paused; he had a hard time talking with his tongue numbed by alcohol. 'The Jewish laws forced Onan to impregnate his brother's wife, and he decided to cum outside of her. He rejected incest and in exchange was named the patron saint of masturbation.'

'That's one thing we agree on,' said Alma, in a serious tone; she seemed upset and the smile had vanished from her face. 'The Bible is a product of misinterpretations, like all bestsellers...'

There was a sudden silence in the room. Alfonso took advantage of it to get their attention.

'You want to hear me talk about masturbation rituals? I've got a story that might interest you...'

X

The phallus was the true cradle of civilization. The Greco-Romans worshipped Priapus, god of fertility, who was always depicted with a huge erection. They put him in their gardens to ensure good harvests and ward off thieves and the evil eye. In the famous frescoes of Pompeii, Satyr and Pan show off their anthropoid cocks to all visitors. In Corsica idols have been found in the shape of a two-meter-tall penis dating to 4000 B.C. The Chinese, Phoenicians, and Assyrians depicted their gods as phallic entities. The Egyptian cross symbolized the penis and testicles. Even the always glum and prudish Catholic Church in its early days came to accept allegories of saints with huge erections, and in many temples there were relics of penises on display. Every culture, in fact, has masturbatory rituals; some in secret, others public. In Africa, young men of the Kikuyu tribe demonstrate their sexual education by masturbating in front of their elders; in some indigenous populations of Colombia it is still customary to welcome guests by handling their genitals; in other primitive tribes men dig a hole in the ground and literally copulate with it to make it fertile . . . And without going any further, my cousins, their friends, and I masturbated as a group. In fact, we had a competition that consisted of seeing who ejaculated first. Or sometimes it was who shot their spunk the farthest. The winner would walk away with the money our parents gave us to buy candy, pooled in advance and kept in a shoebox. The tournament started in an odd way: we played with ourselves while looking at ads from magazines like *Vogue* or *Cosmopolitan* showing women posing in lingerie; the type of publication our mothers would casually leave on the coffee table. I know it's silly, but we didn't have anything better at hand. Afterwards we would line up toe-to-toe along an imaginary line, with our pants around our ankles and our budding erections squeezed between our fingers, and we'd close our eyes in an attempt to call to mind the fantasies that would make us cum before the others. All this took place in the basement, while upstairs in the dining room the adults would be passing around aperitifs, cookies, and coffee at their Sunday family gathering. What I'm telling you about was the normal routine once I was an accepted member of my cousins' and their friends' masturbation club, but there was an initiation ritual I had to go through before I was accepted. The first time I masturbated along with them, they let me win. I hadn't yet gotten over my surprise, panting and excited at having won on my first try, when suddenly the rest of the cocks pointed in my direction and shot their jets of semen on me. Spunk got on my T-shirt and my thighs. In my hair and on my face. On my already flaccid dick. I remember that I cried, that I had to wash it off, that they loaned me clothes so I could go back home, and that I told my mom a story about getting covered in dog shit while playing soccer. But that first day wasn't the source of the real trauma; that came from all the times I took part in the initiations, how much I enjoyed defiling others, feeding off their innocence, spoiling their moment. There was no lust in those acts; maybe in retrospect that would have been less disturbing. It was pure wickedness. Since then it never ceases to frighten me, the knowledge of what I'm capable of.

XI

Someone knocked on the door. They all looked at each other expectantly, but no one said a word. Instead, Ismael imagined how this could be the beginning of a novel: four people isolated in a cabin in the dense darkness of the woods, talking around a fire. Suddenly they receive an unexpected visitor . . . The knocks came again, this time louder, so Ismael set his tequila glass down on the table, got up from his chair, and crossed the room. Before opening the door, he thought: 'And that visitor is an old friend, long dead.' The icy air froze his face. It was the caretaker of the place, who had brought more wood for the fire. Ismael could hardly move his lips to thank him. He took the bundle, closed the door, and went back to his place by the fire. He went on imagining: 'It's a friend they all killed together. But the dead man doesn't want revenge. All he wants is to spend the night talking with them because he feels so alone.' He rubbed his hands together and emerged from his daydream.

'With this wood we can stay up till dawn telling stories,' he said, as he felt the heat return his face to its human form.

'It's Alma's turn,' Ignacio commented. 'I wonder if her story will be free from the semen overload that's been the common thread of ours.'

'The better question is this,' Ismael chimed in. 'Can our

civilization rid itself of that? Alfredo has made it pretty clear that it can't.'

'Don't pin that responsibility on me. Remember, Ignacio is the expert . . .'

Alma stared at the fireplace. Without taking her eyes off the fire, she said:

'We'll see if my story can avoid that. But for starters, it's something different: it's a ghost story.'

'That's it,' thought Ismael. 'The main point of the novel could be the following: ghosts don't do anything to you, but they never leave you. The damage they cause isn't physical, it's mental. They're a psychic contagion, the most powerful kind of all because there's no cure for it.'

And Alma began her story.

XII

In my house there was always talk about superstitions. Around the lunch or dinner table, family legends were told over and over again. How grandpa had heard the Weeping Woman one night. How grandma had seen a shadow looming over the house the day her sister died. How a relative had searched for the Cristeros' buried treasure and had found, in addition to gold coins, the ghosts who jealously guarded them. How my mother had witnessed a virgin crying blood in a village church in the Jaliscan Highlands. We never saw the Weeping Woman with our own eyes, much less the jewels of the treasure, but we all listened to those stories with fascination. Every now and then there was talk of someone who had been 'ridden by the corpse'. It's what happens when you wake up in the middle of the night unable to move. The protagonists of those stories were only acquaintances of the family, until it wound up happening to me. One night around my seventeenth birthday, I started experiencing it. And if it's happened to you, then you know the horror of what I'm talking about: you're totally conscious, but unable to move any part of your body. You have trouble breathing and feel a pressure on your chest. As if someone was indeed on top of you, pinning you down with great force. And at that moment you remember the stories and think that what's squashing you is in fact a dead man. Since speech isn't possible, you don't know what he wants or why he's there. And you lie there frozen while time drags on agonizingly. The most terrifying part is that you can't even scream. When I told my mother about it the next day, she took me to church to pray. But that didn't do me any good, so I told one of my aunts, who was my confidante and who, being the youngest of her siblings, had a different opinion about the stories that circulated in the family. She took me in secret to see a psychologist. After I told him what had happened to me, the man explained that there was a name for the phenomenon: sleep paralysis, and that it occurred during a stage called REM, just before waking, when the brain generates more activity but at the same time blocks the motor neurons. He also told me that it could be caused by a recent trauma and asked me if there was anything like that. I answered him honestly that there wasn't. When the session was over, my aunt agreed to another appointment, but it was almost exam time and I couldn't make it back to the psychologist. A few nights later it happened again. Once again there was the same oppressive feeling, but above all despair at not being able to escape. However, this time there was something different. In the midst of the darkness something took shape for a few seconds. What was on top of me showed its face as if in a flash of lightning. The most terrifying thing I've ever seen. It didn't belong to a corpse. It was the panting face of my father.

★

XIII

Alma raised a hand to her mouth and broke into tears. Then she got up, walked across the room, and locked herself in the bathroom. Ignacio stood up too, ready to console her, but Ismael stopped him with a sign: better to leave her alone. Alfonso poured the last drops of tequila into his glass and finally got around to lighting his cigar. A thick cloud of smoke floated around them like fog from the woods. Minutes later, Alma emerged from the bathroom and returned to her seat.

'I'm fine,' she told them, forcing herself to smile. 'I thought I'd never be able to talk about that.'

'It's all right,' said Ignacio. 'Like we said, none of this leaves here.'

Ismael gave a deep sigh. He had been keeping something in all night and now it was time to let it out.

'It's been really moving hearing all these stories, really, especially since they belong to the darkest corners of ourselves. But I'm surprised nobody's mentioned the *episode*. It's something we've been avoiding ever since we got here. All of us saw Teresa at dinner, don't tell me it didn't surprise you.'

'Surprise us?' Alfonso exhaled the smoke from his cigar as he spoke. 'She was cleared on all charges and released two weeks ago, why shouldn't she be here?'

'Remember,' said Ignacio, 'that very few of us witnessed *that*. Most of our classmates have no idea it happened.'

'But everybody knows she was accused of killing her two kids,' Ismael went on. 'And that didn't stop her from coming.'

'Don't you understand?' Alma got to her feet. 'She came to show her innocence . . . I don't want to keep talking about this. I'm tired, I'm going to bed.'

'I'll walk you back to your cabin.' Ignacio got up too and, addressing the others, said, 'See you tomorrow.'

'I'm going too.' Alfonso pointed to the bottle to show it was empty. 'Tomorrow we'll buy more tequila in the village.'

The three of them went out into the cold wind in silence and shut the door behind them. Ismael knew he wouldn't be able to sleep. Since the *episode*, which took place more than twenty years ago, none of them had stopped thinking about Teresa, and much less could they do it that night when they were so close to where it had happened. Ismael settled in his chair and, surrounded by the ghostly shadows the fire cast on the walls, sank into his memories.

XIV

In the dark of the woods all creatures are possible because you can't see anything. Alfredo knew that was the basis for the mythologies of many of the ancient cultures he had studied. The power of darkness as the origin of atavistic fears. The dead of night that levels us all, prehistoric and modern men, because the fears it produces are the same. There he was, lying in bed, with the covers pulled up to his chin and the oil lamp still burning on the dresser. On the way to his cabin, after walking Alma and Ignacio to theirs, he almost got lost. There was no electric light there and the caretaker had extinguished the torches that lit the paths a while earlier. What scared him most was the idea of meeting Teresa in the middle of that black hole. Their own mythology. The one belonging to the small group who witnessed the *episode*. And now they had returned as if on a pilgrimage to the mountains of Tapalpa, proto-men trying to recognize their own traces in the cave paintings. They weren't in exactly the same place, they would have to walk three kilometers towards the old Jesuit house for that. It would probably be abandoned and in ruins now. He remembered it perfectly. It was really a small school. It had two buildings, three stories each, with a lawn between them. In one of them were the chapel and the classrooms where various activities took place, and in the other were the dormitories and kitchen . . . The kitchen, the epicenter of the chaos that night. No one was able to eat breakfast or lunch the next day, and the retreat had to be cut short a day earlier than planned. They rode back to the city in the school bus in total silence, in contrast to the way there, when they had sung along to rock music blaring from a boombox at full blast while constantly making fun of the driver. Although only a few of them witnessed the *episode*, the rest of their classmates lived it from their rooms, where Joel – the Jesuit in charge of the retreat – had told them to lock themselves in. Alfonso had to leave and reenter the kitchen several times during the *episode*, so he knew that Teresa's screams were audible throughout the whole building. First he went to look for the first aid kit. Then, when Teresa's condition worsened, Joel asked him to go to the assembly room to contact the village, but the radio wasn't working. There was a van, in addition to the school bus parked outside the house, but moving Teresa to the village was out of the question. When he got back to the kitchen, Ismael, Ignacio, and two of their other classmates were struggling to keep her pinned to the table. Teresa had scratched her face, and blood was flowing down her cheeks. She had also torn her blouse, leaving her breasts exposed, but the others didn't seem to notice this detail. Despite the situation, Alfonso couldn't help looking at them: they were much larger than he would have imagined. As if reading his mind, Teresa raised her head and looked at him with dilated pupils. The self-inflicted wounds on her face made her look like she was crying blood. With a voice that wasn't hers, Teresa said to him: 'You like my tits, you little bitch? Come here. I'll feed you my milk like you're a saint.'

It was then that Joel put a hand on his shoulder and, his face marked with despair, told him: 'Go to the chapel and get the holy water.'

XV

Alma knew perfectly well why she had been called to the kitchen that night: she was Teresa's best friend. As she took off her makeup in front of the dresser mirror by the light of the gas lamp, she remembered the last image she had of her before the *episode*. It was the morning of that horrible day, when Teresa and some of her friends were practicing the play they would be putting on two days later as the retreat's final event. Teresa had had a hard time convincing them to take part: they were more interested in running off to the woods with some boy than wasting time memorizing their lines, which Teresa herself had written. Oddly, Teresa wasn't interested in the boys in her class. At least not in the way Alma and the other girls were. For her they were a potential audience. Her world was acting, she had taken part in all of the drama club's performances and had written several monologues. The night before, during dinner, Teresa had obstinately tried to convince her to act in the play. But Alma wasn't so sure she wanted to continue acting. She had shared the stage with her in some end-of-the-year shows, but at that moment her mind was busy thinking of how to repeat her encounter with Ignacio from the previous retreat. Teresa got angry and stormed off to her room, but the next day she acted like nothing had happened, smiling brightly as she rehearsed on the lawn with her half-hearted cast. Maybe that was what shocked her most about the *episode*: having seen her so happy right before it. A few hours later everything changed. She lost her best friend, and for a long time she blamed herself for not having agreed to take part in that play that was never performed. Something inside her told her that her refusal had somehow set off Teresa's transformation. Before she entered the kitchen that night, Joel prepared her: 'It's not Teresa,' he told her, as the sound of a wolf howling came from the other side of the door. 'You have to help us get her back.' When she went in, the first thing she noticed was the intense heat. They were all sweating profusely and their faces were a mixture of exhaustion and fear. She heard a strange voice which she thought at first belonged to one of her classmates. It wasn't until she dared to look at Teresa that she realized it was her speaking. 'Fucking whore!' her friend screamed at her, as the others restrained her with great effort. 'You're here to drink your lover's cum! You want to suck Ignacio's cock in front of everybody, you nasty pig!' Teresa spat a thick wad of phlegm that landed right on her cheek. Alma stood paralyzed. Not just because of what she was seeing, but also because of what her friend had said. There was no way she could have known about Ignacio. She hadn't told anyone about him.

XVI

There were still some embers burning in the hearth when he came to. Ismael rose from his chair, got some logs, and rekindled the fire. Would the others be thinking about Teresa too, like him, or would they have fallen asleep immediately, anesthetized by the tequila? There were a number of things he still found disturbing about the night of the *episode*, but one in particular was beyond his understanding. He was well aware of the power of the mind, what auto-suggestion could do in a sick psyche – and in the minds of those close to its influence. He had seen unsuspected things emerge from the cellars of the unconscious, but something happened during the *episode* that went beyond all logic. At some point that night Teresa grew calmer. She seemed to have fallen asleep or fainted, and her body relaxed on the kitchen table. In that calm interlude, those gathered there became aware of everything that had come out of Teresa's body during her prolonged attacks and convulsions: her clothes were stained with a mixture of vomit, sweat, saliva, and blood. She had also urinated on herself. Alma helped them to clean her up, and they covered her with a blanket. Then they tidied the kitchen: there were dishes and chairs thrown on the floor, broken plates and glasses. Ismael remembered having seen objects flying of their own accord, but he attributed it to the stress of the situation. To the infection spread to all of them by Teresa's mind that night. Once the kitchen had been cleaned and tidied, Joel told them to kneel and pray. Ismael was exhausted and had never believed in prayers, so he sat down in a chair and fell asleep, lulled by the Jesuit's litanies. And he dreamed. He dreamed of the girl who was lost in the woods and met herself in the doorway of a cabin. The dream seemed to contain an enigma or a warning, like some of the stories he had read as a child. But he never found out because his sleep was interrupted. As the girl was walking along the path after saying goodbye to herself, he was awakened by noises and shouts. Teresa was standing on the kitchen table, her back folded backwards in an abnormal position. Her dangling hair almost touched her calves. Her eyes were rolled back and she was mumbling phrases in an unintelligible language. The others knelt again and their prayers grew more intense. They had lit candles in a circle around the table. It was a grotesque scene; it seemed as though they were praying to a twisted god. Ismael only had two choices: kneel or leave. But he did something he didn't expect: he covered his face with his hands and started to cry.

XVII

Ignacio didn't go to bed. He sat on the doorstep of the cabin, peering into the night. The pine trees rocked in the wind in a single, shapeless mass, like primeval gods of darkness. He knew it was no use hiding or locking the door; there was no escape from Teresa. It didn't matter whether they were there in the woods or in the city: Teresa lived in their minds like a presence. He thought about his wavering faith and also how all religion was founded on a traumatic act; at least that was the case in the Catholic Church. The crucifixion as founding myth of a religion based on guilt and the mortification of the flesh. On the conversion of its members into faithful worshippers of nails and wounds. No one dared to look at it like that, but it was the truth: Christians worshipped one of the undead. It was curious and perverse at the same time: Teresa, always so desperate for attention, in her own way created her own religion. The night of the *episode* something began to take root inside him, and by a couple of years later he was in the seminary. Our traumas define us much more than our happy moments, he thought. They're the real revelations about ourselves. The question was: was it really worthwhile to face them and eliminate them, as the healers of minds preached? While she was convulsing on the kitchen table, Teresa had let loose a powerful energy that permeated all of them. At some point she managed to escape the hold of those pinning her down, and half of her body slid towards the floor; her head touched the floor with her arms extended: the inverted cross. Ignacio saw the power of evil and decided to fight it alongside the Jesuits, the only religious order whose members really understood earthly temptations. How could you fight vice if you didn't know it firsthand? He always admired them for that, and he delighted in the story of their expulsion from the New World in 1767: they were the rebels of a Church as interested in sinners as in their wallets. Now he had doubts, and he knew perfectly well why. It wasn't really his faith that was the problem, it was having to choose between two paths. He had come all the way here to get closer to the crossroads. The time of waiting was coming to an end. The night of the *episode*, Teresa made it very clear to him. Before she fainted for the last time, before it all ended and the next day she woke up with no memory of what had happened, she looked at him

with the eyes of a nocturnal animal and in that unrecognizable voice, said: 'We will meet again. Hell is here.'

XVIII

Alfredo had an explanation for the *episode*. He had formu-
lated it over the years, and his studies in the Department of
Anthropology as well as his later field work helped confirm
it. His theory started to coalesce when he did his master's
thesis on religions of possession in Africa and Brazil. The first
thing that caught his attention were the similarities with the
Catholic Church; not in their rituals, but in their conception.
Ancient medico-religious sects saw illness – of any kind – as
divine punishment. Sickness was thus prohibited. And the
rite of possession was used to convert laws that were basically
dictated and applied by humans into signs from above. The
most significant aspect was how these tribes used the notion
of the body as a way of understanding the world. As one of
his professors had told him: 'To the aborigines, the world is
little more than their body.' The Catholic Church synthe-
sized all this in a much more practical and highly evolved way
using the rite of Communion. In other words, the followers
of Christ received his body and spirit – became possessed –
and in this way they 'cured' their soul of sickness; that is, a
conceptual order of the world was transmitted to them.
It was obvious that if belief in the spiritual universe didn't
exist beforehand, religions of possession weren't possible.
Alfredo's thesis was that there was a cultural construct of possession inherent in all religions believing in an afterlife, and
that had created a process of contamination from one to the
other, predetermining the way a possessed person was supposed to act. There was a basic rule, noted by Métraux: 'The
one who goes into a trance is obliged to play the game until
the end.' All of that was very clear to him. He had even grad-

uated with the highest honors. So why at this juncture was he still so scared of Teresa? Why hadn't he been able to get the *episode* out of his mind? It seemed to him that everything he had experienced since then was a consequence of that night, even his choice of career. Maybe that was what was making him panic: not feeling like he was in control of his own destiny. Nothing had happened on its own, it had been caused. Looking at the faint light from the gas lamp in the cabin he dared to admit what he already knew: he was just a puppet in Teresa's diabolical theater.

XIX

When she finished taking off her makeup, Alma put out the gas lamp and lay down, but she couldn't close her eyes. She remembered her student days at drama school, before her professional life became filled with commitments on stage and touring made her work exhausting. What she had liked best was studying: not styles of acting, but the history of the theater itself. In many of the books she read at that time she found answers connected with the *episode*. Especially in a chapter devoted to Greek theater. There it was described how, in ancient Greece, possession rites were closely linked to the emergence of theatrical genres like the dithyramb and the satirical drama. The dithyramb in particular was a feast in honor of Dionysus, made up of a procession of dancers representing the satyrs – companions of Dionysus and demonic and phallic figures *par excellence* – chanting monotonous songs and seeking ecstatic intoxication. There were people in disguise, animal sacrifices, and, above all, a need to reach dionysian ecstasy. The dithryambs contained the fundamental premise of theater – and of all possession – there were the actors, but there always had to be someone watching. Religion, ceremony, and worship were the concepts behind it.

Dionysus, besides being the god of wine, was the one who inspired ritual madness. As some experts, including Hillman, have noted, the complicated nature of Greek polytheism foreshadowed the psychic disorders of modern man. The Catholic Church, always suspicious and opportunistic, had tried to simplify all this, and now its followers were unaware of what the other authors Alma read had claimed: that the rite of Communion was influenced by the cult of Dionysus. He was the only Greek deity who was felt *inside* his followers, and what's more he turned water into wine ... Teresa was always carrying around books on mythology; she must have known about those ideas long before Alma. For Teresa, the theater was a religion. And she did nothing more than seek disciples. There was no doubt in Alma's mind: that night Teresa had put on a grotesque scene, a satirical performance whose goal was to show her the power of acting, to convince her to follow that path. And she had succeeded.

XX

Opisthotonus. It was the medical term referring to Teresa's impossible posture the night of the *episode*. Ismael learned it during his time in medical school. It was something that happened to people with a severe case of tetanus. The muscle spasms and stiffness caused by the bacterium *Clostridium tetani* made the body bend backwards, in the form of an inverted C. A 19th-century painting by the Scottish painter and doctor Charles Bell portrayed this suffering in a dramatic way. But there was one small detail: people suffering from this affliction were in the very advanced stages of the infection and generally could not be cured. The patient died in the majority of cases or was left with terrible lesions on their spine. Obviously Teresa wasn't infected with tetanus. Her opisthotonus had been caused at will – or at least so it seemed. The following day her posture was back to normal. There were, of course, other ways of explaining Teresa's behavior. Psycho-analysis offered several, but the one Ismael found especially interesting was that of Freud, who in his time had dealt with what he termed 'demonological illness'. The Austrian doctor attributed cases of possession to hysteria and neurotic fantasies caused by a severe trauma, usually tied to the absence of the father figure. For Freud, demons or 'psychic beings' originated in 'the interior life of the sick, where they dwell'. Ismael knew that Teresa had lost her father in a car accident when she was little. Shortly after being admitted as a psychiatrist, he thought of looking for Teresa and offering her free therapy to explore the paternal loss, and even figured he could make her relive the *episode* under hypnosis. However, he soon gave up the idea because he realized that it made him feel as though all his years of study had been done with no other purpose than to keep thinking about her, that her shadow was a bigger influence than he was prepared to accept . . .

The demon as a father substitute, he thought as he threw another log on the fire. But there was also the opisthotonus. There were things that had no rational explanation. On that threshold lived creatures like Teresa. And he no longer had weapons to continue fighting. Ismael realized he had come to surrender.

XXI

The world's problems start when things can't be seen clearly. That's why darkness represents an ancestral threat. In his years as a priest, Ignacio had tried to divide the areas of the soul like they had taught him: good and evil, day and night, but the world didn't really work that way. There were too many shades of gray. Contrary to what the Catholic Church preached, fleeing the darkness wasn't the right way: you had to enter it, let your eyes get used to the dark, because learning to see through the night was the only way to perceive the true nature of things. The Catholic Church had a history of ambiguity, however hard they might try to get rid of all the evidence. The first saints, for example, had behaved in a way very similar to the possessed. They ate insects, pus, vomit, and even excrement, in their zeal for self-mortification. The difference was that the saints attained ecstasy by wallowing in filth. This and other details had not escaped even some artists. Why did virgins in some New Spanish paintings suckle saints with a stream of milk directly from their breasts? He couldn't think of anything more perverse. In the realm of twisted things, the medieval brotherhoods of flagellants held a special place: they dedicated themselves to the worship of the Immaculate Conception and whipped their bodies in the aim of transforming them into the virginal body of Mary, in an act of mystic transvestism that sought to erase original sin. Several scholars mentioned it, among them Roudinesco: by dint of resorting to excesses and transgressions, the flagellants ended up being seen as possessed by the demonic passions they were trying to subdue. There was also the case of Ludivina Schiedman, the Dutch mystic who remained prostrate in her bed for thirty years and whose story Ignacio studied with fascination. Obsessed with the idea of saving the Church's soul, she became an authentic possession case: she had wounds, epilepsy, and even dislocated several limbs of her own accord. As she didn't die, she was suspected for a while of heresy. Years later Pope Leo XIII canonized her ... At the seminary they taught him that the line between good and evil was very thin, and for that reason he had to remain stoically on the side of the light. But that was false, cliché and cowardice. Now he was sure that his crisis of faith didn't come from the doubt of whether God existed but from the growing certainty that God and the Devil were one and the same. It was a mistake thinking there were two paths. There was only one.

Ignacio closed the cabin door and walked with firm steps into the darkness.

XXII

The logs burned up until there was nothing left but embers. Ismael didn't feel like throwing more wood on the fire. Nor did he want to go on thinking about the past; he was exhausted and his stomach felt queasy. He was the one who had set this collective catharsis in motion, and now he didn't have the slightest idea what the next step was. He looked at the clock: it was still a couple of hours until dawn. He wasn't sleepy. He felt as though bolted to the chair, incapable of movement. His body was heavy, but especially his head, as if his nocturnal reflections had solidified in his mind. He watched the dying embers and for a few seconds managed to stop thinking. Suddenly someone knocked violently at the door, pulling him out of his trance. He stood up with difficulty and walked to the door as the blows continued more insistently. He didn't stop to think about what was waiting on the other side. He opened the door mechanically and on the doorstep found Alma and Alfredo, visibly shaken. They didn't have to speak for Ismael to understand what was troubling them: over their shoulders, in the distance, a huge fire could be seen shooting its flames towards the night sky.

'What's going on?' he asked them, without taking his eyes off the fire.

'We don't know,' Alfredo answered, 'but we're afraid the fire will spread all the way here.'

'Where is Ignacio?'

'We went by his cabin,' said Alma, 'but he wasn't there. It looks like everyone left.'

'Everyone? Without us? Wait for me . . .'

Ismael went inside the cabin and came back with a flashlight. 'Let's go and check it out,' he said, switching it on.

The three of them made their way along the gravel path that ran between the cabins. Ismael shined his light towards the doors as he walked: they were all open and no one could be seen inside. It looked like the place had been hurriedly evacuated. Going around a bend in the road, they saw a cabin with the light on. It was the only one lit up, and it stood out in the darkness like an immaculate site. Over the open door there was a ceramic rectangle with the number nine. Alfredo stopped them a few steps from the entrance.

'It's Teresa's cabin,' he told them.

'How do you know?' Alma asked in a quavering voice.

'I was one of the last to arrive. I checked the sign-in sheet.'

In the distance, the column of fire seemed to grow higher.

'Let's go in,' said Ismael. 'It's not like we've ever been able to hide from her.'

He stepped forward and went through the door.

XXIII

There was no one inside. Everything was in order, except for a few odd details: there were no clothes in the closet, nor was a suitcase anywhere to be seen. The bed was made and seemed not to have been used.

'Good,' said Alfredo, 'at least we know now she's gone and doesn't plan on coming back.'

'Don't be too sure,' Alma chimed in. 'I saw her arrive and I remember quite clearly that she didn't have a suitcase.'

'Look.' Ismael was leaning over the nightstand. He picked up a piece of paper and showed it to them. 'It's a letter.'

Alma and Alfredo moved closer to stand on either side of Ismael. The three read in silence:

Dear Alma, Ismael, Ignacio, and Alfredo:

I'm sorry we didn't get to see each other, but this is how I decided things would go. Before you try to find me, I have to clear up something important. I know you think I killed my children. But I assure you it wasn't like that, because those children I killed with my bare hands, by drowning them in the toilet, were not my children. You four are my real children, as you will have realized by now. I made you that night more than twenty years ago. You are who you are thanks to me and represent my most perfect little children. But I have to leave you to go back to the place from which I came. I've taken all of our former classmates with me. A small price to pay. Don't be sorry for them: you four have each other. You must stay together and pray for me. It's your mission from here on out. Spread the good word: the fire walks with me, with you, with all.

With eternal love,

Teresa

Ismael left the letter on the nightstand and walked out of the cabin. He looked toward the fire and tried to imagine a route to get there. Alma and Alfredo joined him. There wasn't a sound; it was as though the nocturnal animals were staying silent to hide from the fire.

'Could it be the . . . ?' Ismael didn't dare say the name.

'I think so,' said Alfredo. 'From the location. It must be two or three kilometers. But we can't go there like this, defenseless. The caretaker has a shotgun in his hut.'

They ran towards the entrance to the cabin complex. As they passed through the parking lot, Ismael shined his flashlight on the windshields of the cars: they were all still there. They went in the caretaker's hut and saw it had been ransacked: the glass case where the shotgun was kept had been smashed. The wooden board where the keys had hung was now empty.

'We'll have to go on foot,' said Ismael.

No one objected. Through the window the fire could be

seen. The old Jesuit house blazed violently beneath the starry
sky.

XXIV

They emerged from the perimeter of the cabins and set out
along a dirt road. There were no cars passing at that hour; it
was just them and the sound of their footfalls on the ground.
They breathed through their open mouths, exhaling puffs
of steam. On one side of the gap they could make out huge
shadows: the set of rocky formations that was one of the
hallmarks of Tapalpa. They had gone there in their student
days to get drunk and climb the stones; on several occasions
they had turned the place into a cemetery of trash and beer
bottles.

'The house is behind the *piedrotas*,' said Alfredo. 'There's a
shortcut this way.'

He lifted one of the wires of the fence separating the road
from the field and signaled to his friends to cross to the other
side. Then, being careful not to cut himself on the barbs, he
ducked his head and put his body through. The three of them
made their way in silence, intimidated by those ominous
presences.

Ismael remembered his drinking binges on the stones, on
cloudless moonlit nights. They had always looked to him
like thinking beings, gigantic wise men who watched them
vomit and piss like someone watches an ant crawling across
his arm. The *piedrotas* had been there before them and would
still be there after them: the true dwellers of the woods. He
had the same impression just then as they passed them on
their way to an uncertain fate. Could nature feel compassion
for mankind? They made him long to be a drunk, carefree
teenager again, to reconnect with the boy he was before the
episode. Legend said that the ghosts of children appeared on

the *piedrotas*, and it was true: they were the specters of him and his classmates, shadows of a dead, distant time. A gust of wind blew and Ismael thought he heard an echo of laughter. He turned up his coat collar and quickened his pace. It must be terrible to see a lost soul, he thought, but nowhere near as frightening as meeting the ghost of yourself.

When they had rounded the stone piles, the fire appeared again before them, on the summit of a low hill. They were only a few meters away. None of them hesitated when they headed towards the fire. Only Ismael turned back to take a final look at the stones: he saw the fire reflected on them and also the shadows of children growing longer in the reddish glare of the flames.

XXV

They got to the top of the hill and saw a figure silhouetted against the fire. It was holding a shotgun. Only one of the buildings of the old Jesuit house was still standing; it was completely engulfed in flames, the window glass had burst, and part of the roof was starting to come loose. Nobody else was there. The three of them approached the figure who was watching the fire in a kind of trance.

'She took them,' said Ignacio, his face contorted. 'She took them all. I got here too late to stop it.'

'Are you saying she locked them inside and burned them?' Alma asked, incredulous.

'No. I'm saying that she brought them here and made them pass through the fire along with her.'

'She really was a demon,' said Alfredo, who was watching the fire with a mixture of fascination and horror.

Ignacio turned towards them.

'Teresa created us that night. Doesn't that make her a god instead?'

'Why did she leave us four?' said Alma, more confused than frightened. 'Why didn't she do anything to us?'

'Because we've worshipped her all these years,' Ignacio replied. His gift for preaching was reawakening from the depths of his being. 'We're the ones who keep her alive. Every religion needs its faithful. And a martyr. When the police arrive we'll say Teresa died trying to save our classmates.'

'There's still a way out,' Alfredo chimed in. 'We have the shotgun. If we kill ourselves, there will be no one left to worship her. It'll be our way of getting rid of her . . .'

'Don't you understand?' Ignacio rebuked him. 'The only way to defeat a martyr is to stop her from sacrificing herself. She's already gone. She won. Besides,' he added, offering them the gun, 'which of you has the guts?'

They looked at each other in silence. No one took the gun.

'Just a minute,' said Ismael, pointing a finger at Ignacio. 'You could have done it: written the letter, left it in Teresa's cabin, then forced everyone to come here. You could have locked them in and burned them yourself. How can we believe you if there are no other witnesses?'

'It's a possibility. But remember that all this has always had to do with Teresa, not me . . . Religions are based on dogmas. All we have are these facts and my word. We have to *believe*.'

The roof of the old Jesuit house collapsed and fell towards the center of the structure. After the crash and cloud of dust, the flames flared up again. A pillar of fire rose above the walls. It looked like the burning bush from the Bible stories.

The four of them fell to their knees and began to pray.

Dream of Me

My house is full of cursed dolls. They're my most prized possessions, the envy of my fellow collectors. I've been collecting them for twenty-five years, from antique shops, bazaars, garage sales, flea markets, and lately even on the Internet. My love for traveling has allowed me to pick them up in different parts of the world. That's why my collection is so precious. Every one of them comes with a legend of being possessed, every one of them has a sinister story behind it. Private and governmental institutions have made me offers to create a museum for them, but I like to keep them close by. It's not about the money. Nor is it because they keep me company. Like every collector, I feel as though those objects belong to me. I've had more than one relative or superstitious friend ask me if I'm scared of them. I always respond that in reality the ghost haunting them is me. As the reader will have figured out by now, I don't believe in hocus pocus; my precious objects have never done anything strange or worth noticing. I think the power of legends is to be found in our psyche. A force granted to them by people, and if you're clever enough to understand it, you can make use of it. My collection has made me famous all over the world. They've done articles on me, interviewed me, and I've been on TV many times. Moments in which I take the opportunity to savor the details of each doll. I've never bought one without a verifiable story behind it. That's what the certificates of purchase, files, and newspaper archives are for. I have it all perfectly documented in my records. A collector is a lot like a detective. And if I'm writing all this, it's because this morning someone came to see me. His name was Lugo. He had a package for me. Somebody contacted him through his detective agency and asked him to deliver it to me. All the dolls I've acquired are ones I've found personally, like a skilled hunter tracking his prey. This is the first time a doll has come to me without my having to track it down.

The package the detective handed me contained a doll more enigmatic than any I've ever had. Her name is Greta.

File no. 13
Name: Carlota
Country: Germany
Maker: Nicolaus Otto
Year: 1924

Kopperlsdorf was the kingdom of dolls: many families in the area made their living from manufacturing them. Their body parts were made in people's houses. Only the heads, the main element, were produced in the factories. The demand was so great that they came to produce a thousand dolls a day. The supervisors went from home to home, pressuring their employees to finish the orders on time. Those who fell behind lost their jobs. That was the fate of Nicolaus Otto. Widower and father of five girls, he couldn't keep up the rhythm demanded by the supervisors and wound up out of work. Soon he started to run short of food. His daughters never stopped crying. To calm them, Nicolaus began making the parts for five dolls. However, he couldn't finish them because the heads could only be gotten from the factories, and he had no money to buy them. One day the sobbing ceased. Worried, the neighbors knocked at the Otto family's door, but no one answered. They decided to force the lock. Inside they found a pool of blood and an exult-ant Nicolaus: he had managed to finish his dolls. 'It worked,' he said, between hysterical fits of laughter. 'None of them are crying anymore.'

Before they took him away, Nicolaus gave each doll the name of one of his daughters. Carlota is the only one that has survived to the present day.

Greta is bald, wears a white nightgown, and looks sad. She comes with no documentation, so it's hard to pinpoint her age, but she doesn't look more than thirty years old. Who sent her to me? What is this absurd message supposed to mean? I don't think it's a joke, and if it is, it's a harmless one. Of course I questioned Lugo exhaustively. And in all honesty he proved to be as surprised as I was. He claimed it had been an anonymous phone call. The money was deposited in his account. The voice – the detective couldn't tell if it was a man or a woman – indicated that a package would arrive that same day, and that he had to locate the recipient, Daniel Moncada, doll collector. And that was exactly what he did. Before he left I decided to counterattack: I offered him double if he'd help me find out who had called him. Lugo accepted. He told me he'd call when he found out something.

I spend all day in my study, sunk in meditations as I gaze at Greta. There's something familiar about her. Maybe it's just that I'm getting used to her presence. From her neck hangs a chain and a plaque with her name. It seems rather large for her size, as if it really should have belonged to a different doll.

My eyelids grow heavy. Fatigue overpowers me, I must have been writing in my sleep. I fall asleep and that's when I hear her speak . . .

File no. 06
Name: Teté
Country: France
Maker: Jumeau
Year: 1899

It was a longstanding custom for girls to demand dolls that looked like them. To satisfy this demand, French manufacturers began producing the most realistic dolls in the world. They were babies who laughed and cried just like real ones. To the point where sometimes parents didn't know whether those sounds were coming from the mouths of their daughters or their toys. Against this background André and Julie ordered a doll to be made for Teté, their beloved only child. The workmanship was excellent; the couple readily paid the sum the craftsman asked. Little Teté was very happy with her replica, she would never be parted from it for a single moment. André and Julie were happy too; they even came to feel as though they had two daughters. That joy, however, didn't last. Teté was struck down by an illness so sudden and devastating that her parents didn't even have time to summon the doctor. In the midst of their grief, they decided they weren't going to lose their daughter. They concealed the truth from family and friends; all they told them was that Teté was delicate. When someone close came to visit them, they would see the little one asleep in her bed, or they would hear her crying from her room. The deception worked for a while. To make it even better, André and Julie put their daughter's hair on the doll, hair they had lovingly saved inside a pillow. As time went by, people began to grow suspicious. The girl never got better. Even stranger was that she didn't grow. No one wanted to make their conjectures public, but family and friends started to keep their distance from that strange couple and their even stranger daughter.

For many years, those who passed by their house at nightfall claimed they could hear Teté crying, and her parents consoling her.

I was awakened by the phone ringing. I delayed in answering it because I was paralyzed with horror. The wall clock showed I'd only been asleep a few seconds, long enough for that voice to penetrate my unconscious. When I dared to move, I went to the phone and answered. It was Lugo. He told me he'd asked a contact at the phone company to trace his anonymous client's call. He had an address and was getting ready to pay a visit. He asked me if I wanted to come with him. After considering it for a moment, I told me yes. I wasn't moved by curiosity so much as fear. Greta was on the desk, her glass eyes open and staring at nothing. With a false expression of innocence that made me uncomfortable and compelled me to leave the study. Now, while I wait on the front porch for the detective's car to arrive, I shudder at the memory of the words Greta spoke into my ear as I was falling asleep. Her voice was barely a whisper, the murmur of dry leaves rustling along the ground.

'Dream of me.'

File no. 30
Name: Hanna
Country: Germany/Switzerland
Maker: Simon & Halbig
Year: 1909

Clockwork dolls were produced on demand. The manufacturers in France, England, and Germany began working closely with Swiss watchmakers, who built the mechanisms that gave the toys life. The dolls walked, danced, or rocked other, smaller babies in their arms. Some even moved their eyes, and there are those who claim that's the reason why nowadays those antique toys give the impression of following us with their gaze. And, if they cause that impression in the 21st century, it's not hard to imagine what effect they had at the dawn of the 20th. This was the case in the city of Lucerne, a spot nestled in the Swiss Alps. Heinz Hermann ordered a special gift for the twenty-first birthday of his wife Erika, who loved dolls. She had several, but none with an internal mechanism. The present showed up early, so Heinz Hermann decided to hide it in the bedroom wardrobe until the date arrived. He locked it up and kept the key on him. Unfortunately, the doll had a defect: every evening at seven, the hour when darkness fell over Lucerne, it would switch on and knock against the wardrobe door for several minutes. Heinz Hermann came home from work around eight, so he never knew of the malfunction. But Erika heard those noises and, believing them to be caused by an incipient madness, didn't dare speak of it to her husband. As the days passed, her mental state worsened: that presence fighting to get out of the wardrobe destroyed her nerves. The toy would activate in different ways: sometimes it would walk, other times it would stomp or simply laugh. 'I'll never be able to have children,' Erika told herself, 'because they would suffer the same illness as me.' Just one day before her birthday, the tormented Erika committed suicide, throwing herself headfirst into Lake Lucerne.

Today, the doll Hanna is usually very quiet. She no longer walks, or dances, because her gearwork is damaged beyond repair. From time to time, however, she can be heard laughing.

The journey was long and brought us to the outskirts of the city. On the way, Lugo asked me why I collected cursed dolls. It's a question I've been asked countless times. I used to have fun making up different stories: sometimes I said it was an old family tradition, or that my ancestors had been dollmakers in the Colonial era. I would even venture a paranormal version – especially when being interviewed by some TV station – claiming I had gifts as a medium and that my mission was to free the souls trapped inside the toys. But at that moment, as the landscape changed to forest, making me feel I was approaching the vortex of a secret with my eyes shut, I decided to tell the truth. I told Lugo that my parents had been prosperous in business and hadn't had much time for me. I was an only child and grew up amid the indifference of the servants. For as long as I could remember, collecting things gave me a place in the world. It wasn't that I related emotionally with the objects: I possessed them, and I could be as cold and calculating with them as my parents were with me. Collecting dolls, in particular, was the perfect revenge. Their previous owners treated those toys like children or siblings, but I returned them to their status of objects. They had a value, a file number. They were bought and sold and their names were registered in catalogs, listed in auctions. I had absolute power: I decided whether they went or stayed with me.

'But why specifically cursed ones?' the detective insisted.

I didn't have to think about it. Night was closing in on us, the wind was bending the tops of the trees forward, as though beckoning us to continue our route. I had never been so honest in my life.

'They're more expensive and thus a better investment.'

The car stopped in front of a gate. Beyond it ran a path, at the end of which rose a huge red brick structure.

'But there's something else,' I added. 'I'm not superstitious. I've never believed in anything. Buying those dolls was more a *spiritual* investment than a monetary one.'

'I don't understand,' said Lugo. I detected a certain nervousness in him, as if our conversation was making him uncomfortable. I liked that. Every storyteller should make his audience uncomfortable, otherwise he runs the risk of leaving them indifferent.

'It was a way of rebelling against my humdrum life. As if deep down I wished something supernatural would happen to me.'

'And has it?'

'Maybe it is happening. Today.'

We got out of the car. Now it was pitch black, but the headlights allowed us to read a plaque on the wall beside the gate.

We were at an abandoned orphanage.

File no. 16
Name: Ginger
Country: United States
Maker: Morimura Brothers
Year: 1919

They say the doll walked into the oven on its own.

Robert had been making bread all day; his wife Carol had gotten sick after the difficult birth, her recovery was slow. When little Emily started to crawl, Robert had no choice but to take an old doll from the trunk and give it to his daughter to keep her occupied. Her mother was against it: she said it wasn't a toy, it was a souvenir from her childhood, it had belonged to a friend, and that friend didn't like anyone playing with her doll. Robert paid no attention, figuring his wife's strange comments were due to her illness, and let little Emily play. Carol continued to protest every day from her bed. One time she explained to Robert that her friend had died at a young age; she kept the doll, but never used it for amusement. 'You shouldn't play with dead people's things,' she warned her husband. But he had orders and clients waiting, so Robert ignored his wife.

One morning, as he was putting the loaves in the oven, he heard his daughter crying in the yard. Worried, he went out to look for her but didn't find her. Returning to the kitchen, he saw an image out of a nightmare: Emily crawled rapidly towards the oven and got inside. Robert screamed and tried to reach her, but peering inside he saw nothing but flames. He fetched a bucket of water and put out the fire, but it was too late.

Hours later, a policeman sweeping out the oven in search of little Emily's remains found the doll as well. The mother was not surprised that it had remained intact.

Now I'm in the living room, sitting on a chair as I write this. I'm doing it to put off going to bed. Because I know that when I fall asleep she'll come to me. Greta is still where I left her before going out: in my study. But as soon as I close my eyes she'll haunt me with that request, a plea and a command at the same time: 'Dream of me.' I don't want that to happen; after the visit to the abandoned orphanage, I sense that what she is going to tell me isn't anything pleasant. Most likely things that I don't know, or that have been walled up in my mind. I've never liked thinking about my childhood, and now a cursed doll has shown up to open the doors of my past.

Lugo took two flashlights from the trunk of his car and gave me one. Then he grabbed a crowbar, forced the padlock on the orphanage gate, and we entered the property. As we made our way along the path towards the red brick building, I could sense something moving around us. I shined my flashlight on the ground and saw it was plastic bags dragged by the wind. That didn't reassure me: they seemed alive, getting tangled around our feet as if trying to keep us from going further. We forced open the front door as well and entered the lobby. There was nothing there but spiderwebs, dust, and a small television that probably belonged to the last security guard. A hallway led us to the central courtyard. Two large blocks of sleeping quarters rose on either side of us.

'Let's split up,' Lugo suggested. I was about to reply, 'Not on your life,' when we heard a door banging at the other end of the courtyard.

'It's the wind,' I said, but the detective didn't hear me because he was already running that way. I hesitated a moment, but I preferred to follow him instead of staying there alone. Opening the door, we found stairs leading down to the basement. We descended with caution, covering our noses: the smell of moisture and mustiness permeated everything. We found several storerooms filled with filing cabinets. Lugo began opening the drawers: the records on the children who had spent time at the orphanage were still inside. I wasn't interested in the files: I pointed my flashlight beam in all directions, hoping to find someone lurking in the darkness.

'Follow me,' Lugo said. 'We're looking for the letter *M*.'

'Why?' I asked.

'Because this has to do with you.'

If I'd been brave enough, I'd have gotten out of there right then. But I was paralyzed, confused. When we're afraid we go back to being a child desperately fumbling for the light switch and managing to do nothing but grope in the darkness. The detective found the drawer with the letter *M* and started going through the records. He found a file with my last name. It was a girl: Greta Moncada.

'Do you know her?' he asked.

'No,' I replied. And then I was incapable of uttering another word, because in the glow from the flashlights I saw her date of birth.

She had been born the same year and the same day as me.

File no. 03
Name: Margaret
Country: England
Maker: Lord Shelley
Year: 1860

Lord Shelley squandered part of his fortune on his favorite hobby: the search for the perfect doll. He made dozens of them with his own hands in the workshops of his mansion, working until the dead of night. He made them life-sized; when he felt they were done, he put them in his garden. Over time his reputation grew and word of his extraordinary work reached all corners of the country. However, no one could discover the secret behind those incredible dolls. As is often the case with prominent and envied people, rumors started to spread. It was said that Lord Shelley held banquets which concluded with a peculiar challenge: his daughter Margaret waited in the garden in disguise; whoever could pick her out among all the dolls would receive the secret of his magic as a prize. But anyone who failed would suffer a terrible punishment: he would be transformed by the Lord into one of his famous toys.

As no one succeeded in winning the challenge, the rumors got worse: Margaret was just another of the dolls. But that was just gossip. The only thing certain was that, as the years passed, the garden of the Shelley mansion continued to fill up with ever more impressive and realistic dolls.

We heard more noises coming from upstairs and decided to investigate. For a moment I felt relieved to be leaving the orphanage basement behind. Coming out into the courtyard, we glimpsed a light on the top story of the dormitory building facing us.

'The utilities are all still on here,' Lugo said. 'There's electricity, the phone call to my office came from here, and no doubt there's water too.'

'Do you really want to go up?' I asked. I wanted to get out of there, although on the other hand the prospect of going back home wasn't at all comforting. Greta and her wish for me to dream about her were waiting for me there.

'Of course,' said Lugo. 'We're in no danger here. Haven't you realized that somebody wants us to find all this? Nobody's out to kill us. At least not until we get to the bottom of all this...'

'What a relief.'

We climbed the stairs of the dormitory. We continued to use our flashlights because the switches we pressed along the way didn't turn on any lights.

'The electricity is only connected up there,' the detective said.

We walked slowly. Trash was piled up on the landings and cockroaches roamed in total freedom. I tried not to step on any: there's nothing creepier than the crunch of an insect in the darkness. We reached the top floor. At the end of the hall was an open door and a well-lit room: an invitation to enter. At that point even I couldn't refuse. We advanced while Lugo uttered one of those phrases typical at such moments, but no less disturbing for all that:

'Is anyone there?'

No one answered. The only sound was the echo of our steps. Then I realized: the worst of fears nests in unanswered questions.

We went into the room. There was a bunk, a small table with food scraps on it, a telephone on the floor. The wall was covered in photos, clippings, documents. It took only one of those images to make me remember and to tear down the barrier that for years had kept me safe from my past: twins, a boy and a girl, posing outside the orphanage with their new parents.

She was hugging a doll. He was smiling. There was happiness and hope on their faces. They thought they were going to be together forever.

Unnumbered file
Name: Greta
Country: Unknown
Maker: Unknown
Year: Unknown

There were two orphan twins living in an orphanage. They were very close and promised each other they would never be separated, that they would only go to a home if both of them could come. That opportunity arrived: they were adopted by a couple who were rich and savvy in business. At first the brother and sister were happy in their new home, but that happiness didn't last long. Their parents worked too much, money was their priority; soon they realized they didn't want both children. They only needed one. The other would have to go back to the orphanage. When they told the children their decision, the girl said it was impossible: she and her brother had made a pact and would leave the house together. Unexpectedly, the boy changed his mind. The comforts he had experienced during that time made him break his promise and he opted to stay. The girl left with tears in her eyes, her heart filled with hate. She returned to the orphanage and never left it. When she grew up, she got a job cleaning the bedrooms. In time she became caretaker of the place. One day the orphange closed, yet she stayed. She would die there, but first she wanted to give one final gift to her brother: the doll that had kept her company all that time. Her brother collected dolls, she knew, but none like this one. She hung her own chain around its neck. Before putting it in the box, she whispered in its ear: 'Dream of me.'

Ever since then, she comes every night to visit her brother. And although he may not like it, they are now inseparable.

Pan's Noontide

For Cynthia Fernández Trejo

Maya had been dreaming for weeks about a stranger masturbating. What bothered her most of all was the behavior of that figure, which always appeared seated on one side of her bed, naked and hunched over, his back covered in hair. She had seen a number of strangers touching themselves in real life, but their lewdness was nothing compared to that of the presence that disturbed her sleep. She couldn't even see his face; however, what emanated from his body was so primitive and elemental that it didn't seem to belong to a human being. For a while she managed to downplay the dreams' importance: she focused on her academic research, hoping the nightmare would go away on its own. Faced with its recurrence, she decided to go to therapy.

'Clearly,' the psychiatrist told her at the third session, 'you feel guilty about not sleeping with your husband, and this is how you're atoning for it.'

Her sex life with Arturo was at a low point, not to say dead; she had caught him more than once jerking off in the bathroom or his study, but the psychiatrist's explanation struck her as too basic, too obvious. Maya didn't feel guilty about denying her husband sex; she felt sad. *The death of desire for the person you love should be represented by a funeral*, she once wrote in her journal. It was the precursor of the other death, the most difficult and painful to accept: that of the relationship.

By the fifth session, Maya considered giving up therapy, tired of the psychiatrist dwelling on Arturo's neglected penis

– if you're so broken up about it, why don't you sleep with him? she was on the verge of telling him – but then something happened. For the first time there was a variation in the nightmare: several women appeared, who stood around the unknown man while he masturbated. They all looked at him with delight.

One of those women was her.

Arturo was aware of Maya's nightmares, although he didn't know what they were about. He saw her tossing and turning between the sheets, restless, a frown on her face. She had always been a sound sleeper wherever she might be: in hotels, waiting rooms, buses, even planes about to take off. It was obvious something was going on. He didn't want to ask: he felt estranged from his wife, but above all, he was afraid the answer would pin the blame on him. It was inconceivable to him that two people living together could become strangers to one another. And yet it had happened to him before, with Nerea. He had thought naively that the experience of his previous marriage would help him have a better relationship with Maya. And it had for a while, until things went inexorably wrong. Arturo felt sure that human beings copied themselves, condemned to endlessly repeat their mistakes. He met Nerea at the University. Maya too. One was his classmate, the other his student.

Now both of them were unrecognizable to him.

People are destined to reproduce the past. That's why Arturo had decided to specialize in classical mythology and ancient folklore: he was convinced that the Archetypes that the gods had represented since time immemorial still exerted a powerful influence on modern man. The ancient deities weren't a model to follow, but there was no avoiding the mark they had left. A number of specialists saw a connection between mythology and disease; in fact, the study of mythology was an essential part of a psychotherapist's training.

Beyond what philosophy and science could demonstrate, it was a matter of logic: if a god was suppressed, sooner or later it would return to occupy its rightful place. And Christianity had tried to erase all the pagan deities by means of assimilation.

Lying awake in the middle of the night, Arthur watched Maya struggle against her nightmares, wondering if he could help her. He knew she had started going to therapy; a terrain he was shut out from, since she refused to discuss the subject with him. He could wake her up, despite the warnings he had heard since he was little: don't yank someone out of a bad dream abruptly because their soul will get left behind. Unlike his mother and grandmother, Arturo was not superstitious, although his studies had led to his knowing almost everything on the subject. He was fascinated by the vein of truth that pulsed beneath the mumbo jumbo: you shouldn't spill salt because it used to be worth as much as gold; in Spanish, you wish a stage actor 'lots of shit' because lots of shit-covered carriage wheels outside the theater meant lots of spectators; you knock on wood because pagan religions equated trees with gods.

Maya might be a stranger in his eyes, but he loved her and didn't want her to suffer. All the same, seeing her given over to this deep, turbulent sleep caused him an inexplicable fascination. Her red, curly hair spilled over the pillow; it looked like fiery snakes coming out of her head. Maya let out a harrowing groan; then she put a hand to her throat like something was choking her. She looked like Medusa waiting for Perseus' sword . . . Arturo reached a hand toward his wife, prepared to shake her, but just then she spoke. He thought she had woken up; she never talked in her sleep. Maya repeated the phrase and then started to snore, more calm now.

She had said, 'My shadow and I are one.'

Since she was a little girl, Maya had stumbled upon guys masturbating in public. It had never frightened her; in the beginning it aroused her curiosity and later, when she had a sex life of her own, it made her feel sorry for them. The first one she saw, when she was seven, was a model that would be repeated, with slight variations, over the course of time: the lonely, compulsive exhibitionist, not very physically attractive, camouflaged in the semi-darkness of a theater or exposing himself in the light of day in a shopping center. The odd part was that she couldn't recall their faces; all that came to her mind were hairy hands or swollen penises with bulging veins, but not their faces or expressions. She had never made a big deal out of it; sometimes she didn't even mention it. One time, when she was a teenager and found someone masturbating in the hall of mirrors at a carnival, she left and told her father. But when he searched the corridors, fists clenched, ready to punish the offender, he didn't find anybody. Her father kept his thoughts to himself, but when Maya saw the doubt on his face she understood that it's better to keep certain things to yourself or people will think you're crazy. So she got used to these encounters, which in reality were harmless. She had mentioned it to Arturo, but he had only said, 'Next time, call the police.'

Maya decided to talk about it in therapy.

'It's a childhood trauma coming to the surface in your unconscious,' the psychiatrist told her. 'You see yourself in the dreams because you want to come to terms with those images that left a mark on you.'

'I've never been afraid of them,' Maya explained. 'They've always seemed ridiculous to me, like a dog humping someone's leg.'

'Did you ever feel turned on, or maybe upset? Other people masturbating is disconcerting because it excludes us.'

Maya considered the question.

'Not then, but now yes. In my dreams . . .'

'Turned on or upset?'

'Intrigued.'

The psychiatrist looked up from his notepad.

'Let's go back to your intimate life. You're not having enough sex, and that's reflected in your nightmares.'

'Sex is never enough, even for someone who's having it hand over fist. I don't think it's that. In fact, I'm starting not to see these dreams as nightmares anymore.'

'What are they then? Erotic dreams?'

Maya shifted in her chair, impatient with this man who didn't understand her. She decided to answer honestly.

'They're a call.'

The police officer took the photos from the envelope and spread them out on the desk. They showed from various angles a severed head with goat horns embedded in the forehead. It had been placed on a rock outcropping in a wooded landscape, and it was surrounded by various objects: a flute, a wooden stick with a curved handle, a rabbit skin, and some pieces of fruit. Arturo studied the images while a growing malaise ran through his body. Years earlier he had seen something similar, in a period of his life of which he had only bad memories. When Officer Mondragón of the Homicide Division had asked him to consult on the case, he had gladly accepted. He never would have imagined that the police would show up at his university office to unclog the pipes of the past.

'It's obviously a ritual killing,' Mondragón said. 'What I want to know is if there's some symbolism that might give us a lead or if we're just dealing with a psycho who thinks he's a conceptual artist.'

Arturo set the photos down and leaned back in his chair. He urgently wanted to get rid of Mondragón and call his friend Silvestre, so he got straight to the point.

'There's a clear reference to the god Pan,' he argued. 'He was half man, half goat, tended flocks with a shepherd's crook and played the pipes. According to the Greek myth, he was wrapped in a hare's skin by his father, Hermes.'

'It's an altar?'

'Looks like it. Did you identify the victim?'

'He was a forest ranger in La Floresta.'

Arturo scratched his beard nervously. Hearing that name had increased his anxiety.

'It's strange,' he added. 'A job that fits with the Pan symbolism . . . Killing him like this makes no sense.'

'Why not?' Mondragón wanted to know.

Arturo looked at his watch to signal to the officer that he needed to get back to work. He ran a hand across his forehead in an attempt to banish dark thoughts, and answered:

'The god Pan was the protector of nature.'

In the car, on his way to meet Silvestre in a café downtown, Arturo was plunged into the past. La Floresta was a community located in the forest, on the outskirts of the city, where Nerea had a house. It had belonged to her parents, who brought her there to spend weekends and school vacations. His ex-wife had grown up in an idyllic environment, surrounded by mountains, trees, and a river. She fed squirrels in the garden and left sugar water for the hummingbirds in a feeder attached to her bedroom window. However, by the time Arturo met her at the university, things had started to change. A number of businesses had set up shop in La Floresta with disastrous consequences, among them a sawmill, a chemical factory, and a bottling plant. At that time Nerea belonged to Arcadia, an environmental group that held constant protests and sought to free the community from those exploiting it.

Once they were married, Nerea and Arturo spent long periods in La Floresta. They wanted to take advantage of the isolation to focus on their respective academic projects. Arturo wrote his master's thesis as well as his dissertation in what had been his father-in-law's study. Nerea, on the other hand, was drifting away from books and classes and increasingly focusing her attention on Arcadia. Nothing mattered to her more than protecting the forest where she had spent half her life. For a while Arturo sympathized with her cause, but when Arcadia's actions started to become more radical, he distanced himself from the place and also from his wife.

'What you're doing is terrorism,' he protested to Nerea on one occasion, showing her an article he had just read in the paper.

Arcadia had broken into the chemical factory overnight. According to the newspaper, they had tied up the guard and destroyed the power plant.

'They're the terrorists,' Nerea defended herself. 'If we don't stop them, soon there won't be any fish left in the river.'

Arturo crumpled the newspaper in his hands, annoyed.

'Don't you get it? You could wind up in prison.'

'Relax. I didn't take part in the operation.'

'They could still tie you to the group.'

'You're the only one who knows I'm part of Arcadia, which means the only one who could snitch on me is you . . .'

The arguments multiplied along with Arcadia's actions. Arturo decided to spend more time in the city. Despite his growing anger, he called the house in La Floresta every day, worried about his wife. For several weeks he kept hoping that she would come to her senses and forget about her activism.

Then the incident at the sawmill happened, and he never saw Nerea again.

Maya kept going to therapy because there was another topic she was interested in tackling: her obsession with Nerea. She wasn't jealous; on the contrary, she admired her. But she knew there was something more: she had been trying for a long time to reconstruct her story, first through the constant questions she asked Arturo, and later expanding her research in the archives of the newspapers that had covered the case.

She had to concede that it was an obsession. On the one hand, she acknowledged Nerea's courage in following her ideals to their final consequences, and on the other, she questioned the way she had washed her hands of her relationship, the way she had ended up disconnected from Arturo. Curiously, she was in the same situation now, which made her feel more connected than ever to Nerea. No doubt about it, there was a bond between them, beyond having shared their lives with the same man. But what was it? That was what she intended to find out.

'You identify with her as a way of justifying your rift with Arturo.' Once again the psychiatrist didn't understand a thing, but it didn't matter: Maya needed to think about these things aloud, tell them to the therapist, even if he was clueless. 'If she failed, it's logical for you to fail as well. The root of the problem, then, is him and not you.'

'She put her own interests above his, she had a very clear objective, that's admirable – ' Maya paused for breath, before making the following revelation to herself: 'On the other hand, I've drifted apart from Arturo for some reason unknown to me.'

'Couldn't it be because you think there's something better out there for you? Arturo is fifty, you're younger.'

Maya had just turned thirty-six, the same age as Nerea when she vanished from Arturo's life. A coincidence she found unsettling.

'Are we condemned to repeat what others have done?' she asked, ignoring the psychiatrist's question. 'Arturo thinks we repeat our own mistakes, but sometimes I think we also copy other people's . . .'

'How was the sex between Nerea and Arturo? I'm sure you know.'

Of course Maya knew. Intense at first, scarce in the end. Wasn't it that way in all marriages? You start off sleeping with your lover, with the person you desire most in the world, and you wind up cuddling with someone who has become, in the best case scenario, your sibling. And in the worst, your kid.

'It went to shit,' she replied. 'Who can make the good things last?'

'The similarities with Nerea keep growing. Neither of you had children, but you still could. Your refusal to sleep with Arturo brings you one step closer to her . . .'

Maya grew thoughtful. She had never seen Nerea, had never even spoken to her. Yet she felt very close to her.

Closer and closer.

Arturo got to the café half an hour before his appointment with Silvestre. He ordered a beer and tried to distract himself by watching the other customers, but it was no use. Soon his thoughts were filled with memories and reflections on his relationship with Nerea. Where did everything go wrong? At what moment did they reach the point of no return? There was no question she underwent a profound personality change; the only way Arturo could explain it was through Arcadia. Nerea's involvement with the environmental group was a negative influence; her relationship with Pedro, Arcadia's egocentric and obnoxious leader, in particular affected her. Arturo never liked his manner; he was annoying and histrionic. He did everything in excess: talk, eat, drink. During his interminable diatribes he would wave his hands and spray saliva. Arturo never could understand what fascination such a repulsive person could have had for his wife. For a while he suspected they were having an affair, but later he realized that what Nerea was experiencing was a sexual awakening that didn't center on a single person.

On one occasion, in the final stage of their marriage, when Arturo had gone back to live in the city, he decided to pay Nerea an unannounced visit. He drove to La Floresta and got there early in the morning; the sun was just peeking over the mountains and the dew shone on the leaves of the trees.

The front door was ajar, so he went in without knocking. On the chairs and hardwood floor in the living room there were several half-nude people. Men and women slept with their bodies entwined after an apparent night of partying: there were empty wine bottles and glasses everywhere. With a mixture of indignation and fear, Arturo made his way to the master bedroom, expecting to find the worst-case scenario: Pedro sleeping in what used to be his bed, with the woman who was still his wife. He pushed the door open cautiously and peeked inside. What he saw surprised him: Nerea asleep in the arms of two very young women, almost adolescents. He backpedaled, disturbed. Nerea had wound up falling into the hippie lifestyle that Arcadia preached. Arturo thought that it wasn't so much an environmental group as a cult. Pedro was the typical leader with messianic airs who used a cause as an excuse to enjoy sexual favors from his followers. Arturo looked for him all over the house; he wanted to give him a piece of his mind, but he didn't find him anywhere.

He decided to leave. He got in his car and headed for the road that led away from the property. A sharp scream from the side of the path caught his attention. At first he thought it was a baby, but what he witnessed unsettled him even more. In a shed used for storing tools he saw Pedro. He was standing there naked, watching in fascination as a cat who had just given birth ate its own placenta.

Arturo found out about the incident at the sawmill on television. The building had burned to ashes in the middle of the night, with one casualty: a technician working a double shift to fix a faulty machine. Although the authorities didn't know what caused the catastrophe, Arturo had a feeling he knew who was responsible. He called Nerea, but she didn't answer. After a few minutes, anxiety got the better of him; he took the car and headed to the house in La Floresta. Arturo knew that over the past few weeks it had become

Arcadia's headquarters. There were strange people coming and going at all hours or spending the night there. When he arrived and rang the doorbell, he realized the place was deserted. Then there was no longer any doubt: the environmentalist group had carried out the attack. He went back home, called in sick to work, and spent the rest of the week glued to the news.

As the days passed, his worst fears were confirmed. The police announced that the fire at the sawmill had been started by a radical environmentalist group and that the investigation was closing in on those responsible. One by one, Arcadia's members were taken down, including Nerea. Arturo saw an image of her on the television screen, her hands cuffed and an arrogant look on her face. That was what bothered him most: she didn't look frightened or sorry. Pedro took all the blame: he claimed he had been the only one at the sawmill and that his aim hadn't been murder.

'There wasn't supposed to be anyone there that night,' he said in front of the TV cameras. 'The worker's death was an accident.'

He sounded sincere. Then he added something that proved to be his downfall:

'In ancient times, trees were considered sacred,' he said, looking at the camera with a fanatical expression. 'And now they're targeted for extermination. Maybe this collateral death will make people wake up. When we kill nature, we're killing our gods too.'

Arturo knew what Pedro meant. The Scandinavians attached great importance to Yggdrasil, the tree that represented the universe; the druids venerated oaks, for the Syrians it was cedars, and the Jews had a cabalistic tree. Primitive sects believed in 'tree men', and the presence of the Green Man of the Celts, with a face made of leaves, could be traced in various medieval constructions.

But what Arcadia had done was unjustifiable. Pagan beliefs

and their symbology relating to natural cycles were one thing, but murder was another. Pedro had let himself get carried away by his convictions to the point of becoming a criminal. And he had dragged Nerea and a group of naive, idealistic young people along with him.

As was to be expected, Pedro received the harshest sentence and was still in prison. Nerea and the other members of Arcadia got shorter terms and, after a few years behind bars, they had regained their liberty.

The sawmill incident marked the end of Arcadia. After she got out of prison Nerea filed for divorce, abandoned the house in La Floresta, and vanished off the map. Arturo kept an eye out for news on environmental topics, in search of a clue to his ex-wife's whereabouts. Later, when Maya came into his life, he realized it was time to let go of the past. For a while, he actually managed to forget Nerea. Until Mondragón turned up and showed him the photo of the decapitated ranger.

Silvestre looked changed. His hair had gone gray, his clothes looked shabby. His image didn't match the man Arturo remembered: elegant, self-confident. What surprised him most was learning that he'd gone into a new line of work: selling insurance. Silvestre had studied environmental sciences and for many years had been a respected academic whose articles were published in specialized journals. The last Arturo had heard, he was working in La Floresta. In response to media pressure, the companies operating in the forest had decided to hire a consulting group, with the promise of reducing their environmental impact. It was around that time that Silvestre showed him a photo similar to Mondragón's: a severed head, surrounded by references to the god Pan. At the time, Silvestre told him he had found it in an archive, and that he was intrigued by its symbolism. Arturo assigned no importance to it and – after giving him the same explanation he gave the cop years later – he forgot the whole thing. But now things were different: he wanted to know where his friend had gotten that disturbing image.

Silvestre looked around, as if checking to see who was sitting at the neighboring tables, and said:

'I have nothing left to lose now, so I'll tell you.'

Silvestre told him how, a few months after joining the consulting committee, he realized it was a fraud. The industries that had hired them – the sawmill, the chemical factory, and the bottling plant – were just seeking legitimacy and a screen to hide behind. Although they set up an office for the consultants in the forest and paid them a considerable sum, they never asked for any reports. Meetings with management were continually postponed. Nonetheless, Silvestre decided to take his work seriously; he began taking long walks around the businesses to collect evidence of the damage they were causing. With the aid of a camera he documented the alarming contamination of the river, the indiscriminate felling of trees, and the exploitation of water resources.

One afternoon as he walked along a path near the bottling plant he stumbled upon a strange sight: a mound of stones with a cloud of flies at the top. When he got closer, he discovered to his horror that there was a severed head. His first impulse was to take pictures of it. Then he went back to the office to report his find. There was nobody there: it was after seven and none of his colleagues stayed past closing time. He picked up the phone and called the police. He waited for them to get there, then led them down the path. To his surprise, they didn't find anything: both the mound and the head had vanished. Silvestre told the police that he had photos and took them back to the office. But the camera, which he had left on his desk, was no longer there. The next day he received an anonymous email. Attached was one of the photos he had taken of the head. The text said: FORGET ABOUT THIS OR WE'LL DESTROY YOUR CAREER. Frightened, Silvestre decided to keep quiet. Shortly thereafter he resigned from the com-

mittee. His departure coincided with an accusation of pla-
giarism from one of his colleagues, and another of sexually
harassing one of his students. Both were falsehoods, but they
worked. The doors of the academic world didn't take long to
close for him.

'Why the punishment, if you heeded the warning?' Arturo
wanted to know.

Silvestre sat staring at a coffee stain on the tablecloth. After
a long pause, he said:

'I gave the photo from the email to one of the tabloids. For
my own peace of mind.'

'And why did you show it to me?'

'That was before I resigned from the committee. I was
really upset, I needed an explanation.'

'And you never found out anything else? Who the victim
was, who had threatened you?'

Silvestre ordered another round of beers and wanted for
the waiter to bring them.

'Years later,' he said, 'when the committee dissolved, a
former co-worker told me about the rumors that were going
around among the companies' employees. The head belonged
to the watchman at the bottling plant, and the killer had been
the owner's son: he was a member of a satanic cult. The father
paid the watchman's family off so they wouldn't talk and sent
his son abroad . . .'

'A satanic cult . . . Do you believe that story?'

'I don't know. People have overactive imaginations. The
truth is, by the time my ex-colleague told me, I didn't care
too much anymore. I was too busy trying to survive.'

Arturo sat silent. People didn't know much about pagan
gods. But he no longer had any doubt: Arcadia was back,
and it was a much more dangerous organization than he had
thought. He closed his eyes and prayed Nerea wasn't involved.

Another image began to recur in Maya's dreams. She saw herself in a landscape of hills and yellow grass. The wind played with her hair and brought her an intense scent of flowers: jasmine, gardenias, lilies. The cloudless sky was a dome of cobalt blue. Maya stood on a gravel road, an old causeway whose path vanished into the distance. Her gaze strayed from the horizon and lowered to focus on a strange phenomenon: her body, lacking a shadow. The sun, at its zenith, hid it. There was an intimidating brightness, a blinding clarity. Nothing else happened in the dream: she never moved from the spot, nor did anyone appear by her side.

It was a mysterious moment, full of omens.

Maya talked about it at her final session with the psychiatrist. She didn't consider it necessary to go on attending therapy: now she knew that the answers lay elsewhere.

'It's not for nothing,' the psychiatrist told her, 'that in the dream a path appears that you don't take. You're afraid of moving forward, discovering new things.'

'I know where that path leads, maybe that's why I don't take it.'

'And where does it go?'

'To a cavern.'

'A shelter?'

'No: a sanctuary.'

The psychiatrist noted something on his pad. Maya still hadn't told him that she wasn't planning on coming back. What would he do afterwards with those useless notes? She took advantage of the pause to add something:

'In the dream I feel intrigued by the absence of my shadow.'

'There are old superstitions about that. Some African tribes are afraid of losing their shadow, so they avoid open spaces at noon.'

'But in my dream I don't feel fear. The shadow's absence is like the announcement of something important.'

'A decision that's approaching, maybe?'

'Or a person.'

Maya looked at the wall clock: the session was over. She got up and headed for the door.

'Wait,' said the psychiatrist. 'It's important for you to talk about all this with your husband at some point. You know that, right?'

Maya nodded. Did the therapist sense she wouldn't be back? In any case, he had left her with the best advice he'd given her in all this time. Yes, she had to talk with Arturo. But first she had to find Nerea.

This time Mondragón hadn't made an appointment. He approached Arturo in the halls of the university and asked him to take a walk with him through the campus gardens. They passed between jacaranda trees, distancing themselves from the groups of students smoking and talking on the lawn.

Arturo spoke in a low voice, afraid his words would be overheard.

'I hope your coming here doesn't mean another body has turned up ...'

'You're a pessimist,' Mondragón said, looking at the students with curiosity, as if they were a different species from him. 'Nobody else has been killed, but it could happen at any time. We checked out the ranger and discovered he had connections to poachers. I wanted to let you know.'

'It's an important piece of information. But you could have told me over the phone.'

'I wanted to see you in person. I was left with the feeling that you know more than you told me last time.'

'What could I be hiding?'

'I'm not saying you're hiding anything, but I think you have your own theory of the case, and for some reason you don't want to tell me.'

Arturo realized the detective was putting him to the test. Sooner or later the name Arcadia would come to light; he had better say something about it or he'd be an accessory. But he wouldn't mention Nerea's name unless it was unavoidable.

'The ranger betrayed his duty,' he said, trying to hide his nervousness. 'Whoever killed him was sending a clear message: nature matters more to them than human life.'

'Why are you talking in the plural? You think it was more than one person?'

Arturo had made a mistake. And now there was no going back.

'In La Floresta there have been groups of radical environmentalists,' he replied. 'A few years ago, there was an attack on a sawmill and somebody died. But I suppose you already know that . . .'

Mondragón reached into his inner jacket pocket, took out a clipping, and handed it to Arturo. It was a page from an old tabloid. The notice was accompanied by the photo Silvestre had taken of the severed head. The headline said: SATANIC RITUALS IN THE FOREST.

'I think both crimes are related,' said Mondragón.

Arturo read the story and handed it back to the policeman.

'Someone is taking their beliefs to the extreme.'

Mondragón stopped in the shade of a jacaranda.

'Are we dealing with a group of satanic environmentalists?'

Arturo couldn't conceal a look of disappointment.

'That's one way of putting it. Although it's not exactly the right term . . .'

'Please explain.'

'Whoever committed these crimes worships the ancient Greek god Pan. A figure assimilated by Christianity, adding his attributes to the Devil: the horns and hoofs of a male goat. Pan was not an evil deity, but if you made him angry, bad things could happen. I'm afraid this case involves beliefs much older and more enduring than belief in the Devil.'

'Do you believe in the Devil?'

Arturo felt overwhelmed by the conversation. He raised his face in search of fresh air, but the purple of the jacarandas struck him as painfully intense.

'I'm an atheist,' he replied. 'However, the original gods make more sense to me. What's more, the Devil is an invention used to establish a moral code. The god Pan signifies something more disturbing: he represents nature, and therefore instinct.'

Mondragón looked uncomfortable too. It was obvious the subject was beyond him.

'And what does that mean?' he asked.

Arturo chewed on his response.

'Maybe the Devil lives inside some people,' he said. 'But without a doubt there's a god Pan inside every one of us.'

For the first time in years, Arturo resolved to go to the house in La Floresta. He had to check it out. He drove slowly, taking the long route, deliberately delaying the moment he would have to face it. Two hours later he parked outside the property. He stayed in the car for several minutes while debating with himself whether what he was about to do was a good idea. Finally he made up his mind and got out of the vehicle. The grounds were surrounded now by a chicken wire fence, which looked old and some sections of which had even collapsed. Arturo looked around and, taking advantage of the fact that nobody was passing by, slipped inside. The road leading to the house was overgrown with grass, and there was trash strewn all along his path: empty beer bottles, potato chip bags, the remnants of campfires. He felt a stab of pain in his stomach when the building appeared before him. The peeling paint and boarded-up windows evinced a long neglect. He stopped at the door and took out the key, which for some absurd reason he had kept. He hoped it wouldn't work. Then he would turn around and leave, with the peace of mind of knowing he had tried.

To his surprise, the lock gave a click and then turned. Arturo pushed the door open and stood in the doorway, undecided. He tried to figure out how many years it had been since he'd set foot in the house. Ten? He sighed and took a step forward. The interior was in a semi-darkness in which the shapes of things could be made out. The furniture was covered with sheets. It smelled musty, but there was another smell too: a thick, sweet aroma that he couldn't identify. The pictures were still on the walls, the knickknacks on the shelves, and the books on the bookshelves, covered in dust. He walked through the ground floor. There was a hole in the board covering the dining-room window; a ray of sunlight passed through it and fell onto the table. On its surface he discovered the source of the odor: there was some fruit start-ing to go rotten. Three green apples – Nerea's favorites, – a papaya, and a bunch of bananas. Somebody had been in the house recently.

Along with the fruit there was something else: a wide rec-tangle of paper with drawings and notes. Arturo leaned over it. He studied it and realized it was a map of the city sewer system. Instinctively he took it, folded it in two, and put it in the inner pocket of his coat. Then he left the house with hurried steps. He was afraid the map's owner might return at any moment.

From the first sessions, the psychiatrist had advised Maya to keep a dream diary. She refused while the therapy lasted, but now that she was no longer going she decided to try it. She went to a stationery shop to buy a notebook. She liked horses, so she picked one with a collection of manes on its cover. What's more, it struck her as meaning something: dreams are like wild horses that, no matter how much you mount them, never allow themselves to be tamed. Where should she start? With previous dreams or the ones she would have starting that night? After thinking about it, she decided to start from zero. She kept the notebook in the drawer of the nightstand: she didn't want Arturo to find the diary and start asking questions. Although, now that she thought about it, her husband had stopped asking questions a long time ago. It was obvious he no longer cared what she thought. In any case, protecting her privacy seemed important to her. At least for the moment. She shut the drawer and locked it. The next morning she would write down the images from that night.

Then she went on with the work she had been busy with in recent days. She got out her phone directory and started calling old acquaintances from the university, in search of a lead as to Nerea's whereabouts. The problem was that she had disappeared without a trace; nobody knew anything definite about her. Only scattered bits of information, overly vague: she had signed on to a Greenpeace boat, she had become a missionary in a third-world country, she was an activist in the Amazon. Not to mention rumors that verged on urban legend: Nerea had grown obsessed with the melting of the Patagonian glaciers and had spent years recording the sounds they made as they disintegrated; Nerea had gone mad and founded a cult that lived underground, awaiting the climatic apocalypse . . .

Among all the numbers in her directory, there was one person in particular who might be able to help her: Silvestre, who worked in La Floresta. But Maya left him until last because she didn't want to contact acquaintances who were close to Arturo. If her husband found out she was trying to locate Nerea, he would get angry. And the last thing she wanted was a fight with him.

One time Arturo had reproached her for it.

'Stop poking around in my past,' he told her, raising his voice. 'You're more obsessed with Nerea than I was when she disappeared.'

Maya had felt bad about it, since she knew she was opening old wounds. From then on she was more discreet about the subject, and she set out to compile a dossier with newspaper clippings and videos about Nerea and Arcadia, which she kept hidden from her husband's eyes.

Now she had no other option.

She picked up the phone and dialed Silvestre's number. After a few pleasantries, Maya asked him if he knew where she could find Nerea.

'I know what everybody knows,' Silvestre replied. 'That after getting out of prison, she vanished. Odd that you should ask me . . .'

'Why?'

'Not long ago, Arturo came to see me about an old matter connected with La Floresta. It seems to me that it's the two of you who know something about Nerea, and you don't want to tell me.'

Maya decided to be honest.

'Arturo and I aren't talking much lately. This search is for me, I need to talk to her. Can you tell me why Arturo came to you?'

'I'd better not. If he hasn't told you about it, then . . .'

'Don't hide behind that pathetic male solidarity. You've always been better than that, Silvestre. I don't want to get you into any trouble, I'll be discreet about what you tell me.'

Silvestre pondered for a few seconds.

'All right,' he said at last. 'I'm sending a photo to your inbox.'

The entrance to the cave was outlined in yellow police tape. A couple of officers were in charge of chasing off the reporters and curious onlookers who thronged in search of information. Arturo had had a hard time finding this remote part of La Floresta; he wondered how all these people had managed to get there before him. A police car was parked to one side of the path, along with a van from the medical examiner's office. Arturo went closer, treading the rocky soil carefully.

He elbowed his way through and managed, between jostles, to reach one of the officers. He showed his ID and explained that Mondragón had sent for him. The officer spoke into his radio; after receiving an unintelligible order, he lifted the yellow tape and let him pass.

'Follow the cables,' he pointed, referring to some orange cords snaking along the ground and disappearing into the cave's interior.

Arturo steeled himself and went on. He didn't have to walk far to find the men working inside. Gathered around a stone altar and lit up by three powerful floorlamps, a group of forensic specialists was busy cataloging evidence. He spotted Mondragón among them.

The officer signaled for him to come closer.

'If you feel like you're going to vomit,' Mondragón warned him, 'make sure to do it away from the evidence.'

On the stone altar lay the body of a young man. He was naked and lying face down; there was an enormous gash on his neck, from which a considerable amount of blood had gushed. The red liquid bathed the front part of the altar and formed a puddle on the ground. An object protruded from between the victim's buttocks: a flute, which had been inserted halfway into his anus. Around the corpse was a series of objects: a cup in which some of the blood had been collected, a wooden phallus, and various musical instruments: a violin, a psaltery, more flutes.

Arturo felt queasy. Mondragón noticed it; he took his arm and led him to a distant corner of the cavern.

'You saw enough,' he said. 'What do you think?'

'More references to the god Pan,' he answered, then paused to stifle a retch. 'The instruments, the flutes ... Music was important in Pan worship. And the phallus: Pan also symbolizes sexual compulsion.'

'Why this place?'

'Unlike other gods, Pan didn't have a temple. He was worshipped in grottos, valleys, and fountains – ' Arturo paused while he thought. 'Nobody comes out here. Who found him?'

'Anonymous tip. We still haven't officially identified the victim, but one of the officers says it's the bottling plant owner's son.' Mondragón wiped his forehead with a handkerchief; the lights were making the cavern hot. 'They're not going to stop, are they? The satanic environmentalists . . .'

'I'm afraid they won't. I think what they're going for with these rituals is the return of the god Pan.'

'They're crazy. I'll comb this forest until I catch them.'

Arturo thought of the map he had found in the house in La Floresta and its connection with the city's underground. He didn't want to mention it to Mondragón. He'd made up his mind: he was going to investigate it on his own.

There's a naked woman lying in my bed. I can't see her face because she's covering it with her arms, which she keeps crossed at eye level. Her armpits show black hair. She's let it grow on her groin and legs as well. Her skin is milky and marked with a constellation of moles. The soles of her feet look black, as if she'd been walking through dirt before coming into my room. I know I'm not here to join her but to watch her. She lowers one hand and puts it on her vulva. She caresses her clitoris in circles then inserts her middle finger. I think about how it's women's favorite finger when we masturbate. The woman tilts her head and bites the skin on her forearm; she holds it between her teeth and gently stretches it. That movement allows me a glimpse of her hair, which is brown and smooth. Then she lowers the other hand to pinch a nipple. Her abundant head of hair continues to hide her face. I know that this woman is my mirror image, even though we have different bodies. She's part of me, the same way my shadow and I are one. Her toes tense up; I realize that the most animal part of any orgasm isn't in facial expressions or screams, but right there, in the curling of the toes, like claws trying to grip a tree branch to avoid falling into the void . . .

*

The map had a circle marked in red, which corresponded with the intersection of two streets in the city center. On a first visit, Arturo found that it was a pedestrian thoroughfare and that there was a sewer drain at the intersection. He waited patiently; when there weren't many people around, he bent down, seized the iron cover and, although it was heavy, realized he could lift it with his hands. Then he moved away so as not to call attention to himself. He decided he would come back later, with a flashlight.

At home, Arturo studied the map again and waited for Maya to fall asleep. They hadn't spoken in days, each of them immersed in their own preoccupations.

In the dead of night he went back to the spot a second time. Taking advantage of the streets being empty, he went into the sewer. He climbed down a wall ladder, then stopped at the edge of the canal that transported the sewage. He covered his nose with a handkerchief and started to breathe through his mouth. Then he made his way with caution, shining his flashlight on the floor to light his way. Several rats, fat and black, fled at the sound of his steps. The map had other markings. He had memorized them because he didn't want to bring it with him: in some way he felt that it incriminated him, that it could be used as proof against him.

Or against Arcadia.

He turned to the left at a junction and felt the ground start to slope. He was on the verge of slipping, but leaned against the wall for support. After an arduous walk, which felt endless, the ground leveled off again. He could see nothing but his feet, lit up by the flashlight. Sudden splashing sounds could be heard from the water flowing beside him. He supposed it was rats swimming. He didn't dare imagine anything else. Minutes later, he arrived at an arch and a waterfall that formed there. He searched along the wall and found another ladder. He descended until he reached a small platform. He knew from the map that the course of the water continued to the left, but he had to focus on the right side because there was another mark there. He shined his flashlight around and found a hole in the wall. He stuck his head in and pointed the light into the void. Ten meters down there was a kind of cavern. The beam of light barely managed to illuminate it; however, he could make out some designs on the wall, anthropomorphic figures that seemed to be writhing or dancing in the darkness. He couldn't reach the bottom without a rope. Arturo started back, with a mixture of excitement and fear. He felt he was close to finding Nerea.

Pedro didn't resemble the image Maya had seen in magazines and old TV news reports. He was far from the fierce and athletic figure that had climbed to the tops of trees to keep them from being felled, stoically enduring the tear gas the police threw at him to force him down. He had a thick, white beard, a prominent belly, and a red wool cap on his head. His looked more like a shopping mall Santa than a radical activist whose actions had led to someone's death. The glass separating them in the prison visiting room reinforced that idea, as if Pedro were in a store window during the Christmas season.

Maya decided to interview him after her conversation with Silvestre. The revelation about the ritual murder in the forest pointed toward him: no one else in Arcadia had such a vocation for sacrifices. It wouldn't surprise her if he had gone on pulling the strings from prison to get rid of his enemies.

At first she was surprised Pedro would accept a visit from a stranger, but as soon as they began the conversation through the handset she realized he knew much more than she had imagined.

'You're Arturo's wife,' Pedro said by way of greeting. 'I wondered how long it would take you to come . . .'

'Why?' Maya asked.

Pedro looked at her intensely. There was arousal in his gaze, but different from what Maya had seen in other men. It wasn't that he was undressing her with his eyes: it seemed that Pedro could see inside her, beyond her flesh and guts. Maya felt that this stranger understood her true essence, and therefore it wasn't desire that he was projecting but recognition. Arturo had never seen her that way . . .

'Because you're looking for answers,' said Pedro. 'And I'm part of the puzzle.'

'Are you going to tell me what I want to know?'

'Depends. Try me.'

'Where is Nerea?'

'You're not ready to know that. All in good time.'

Maya hesitated. After her initial impression, she now saw Pedro differently: a charlatan who enjoyed making himself mysterious. She decided to be more aggressive. She took out a printout of the photo Silvestre had sent her and pressed it against the glass.

Pedro ignored the severed head on the altar.

'It seems to me you're looking in the wrong place,' he said.

'Maybe this is the reason Nerea is hiding.'

Pedro leaned forward and put his forehead against the glass. His hairy face and his scrutinizing eyes gave him a primitive, animal appearance. He no longer looked like Santa Claus but a caged predator in a zoo.

'You think you're looking for answers about your past,' he said emphatically. 'But really all of this has to do with your present. And above all with your future.'

Maya put the photo away, disappointed. Coming to see this nutcase had been a waste of time. She was about to hang up the phone, but Pedro stopped her with a gesture.

'You don't have to look for her,' he said. 'Nerea is in your dreams.'

Arthur moved more confidently through the sewer tunnels because now he knew the way. He reached the platform; he tied one end of the rope to the hand ladder and threw the rest into the hole in the wall. Then he put his body through and descended slowly to the bottom of the cavern. Once there, he shined his light on the walls. This time he had brought a larger and more powerful flashlight. What the light revealed was a huge mural depecting the forest. There were mountains, trees, and a river, and also people dancing around a central figure. Arturo went closer to see better. The painting was obviously recent. What was represented in the middle of that pagan celebration was the god Pan, who was fornicating with a she-goat. He recognized the image: it was based on a sculpture from the first century B.C. The goat lay face up, looking into Pan's face while they copulated . . .

He was absorbed in studying the mural when he heard footsteps behind him. He turned around, frightened. He didn't recognize him until he spoke, because he was shielding his eyes from the flashlight with his hand.

'Point that somewhere else or you'll blind me,' Mondragón said.

'What are you doing here?' Arturo didn't know whether to feel relieved or worried.

'Do you think I'm an idiot?' the cop said. 'I've been using you as a decoy all along. I know very well who your ex-wife is.'

'I don't know where she is. Really.'

'I believe you. And now I'll take it from here. If you stick your nose in this case again, I'll charge you with obstruction. Get lost.'

Arturo took a couple of steps towards the rope, then stopped.

'There's something else . . .'

Mondragón was about to call on his radio. With a gesture, he pressed him to continue.

'I was wrong,' Arturo said. 'I thought Arcadia's intention was to bring the god Pan back to the forest, but now it seems clear to me there's something worse going on . . .'

'Worse than decapitating innocent people in ridiculous rituals?'

Arturo nodded.

'They want to bring the god Pan to the city,' he said.

He made his way to the rope, climbed up, and disappeared through the hole in the wall.

He didn't see when the figures emerged from the shadows and pounced on Mondragón.

. . . the place is familiar to me. I'm in Parque Metropolitano, in the heart of the city. A place with pedestrian avenues and huge expanses of grass and trees. It's night. The light of the full moon allows me to get my bearings in this maze of gardens and fountains; I'm walking in the section containing the oldest ones, made of stone and topped with bronze sculptures representing ancient Roman gods. In the one dedicated to the god Faun a woman bathes while singing a song. I can't make out what language she's chanting the verses in, but I understand that it tells of primeval forests and the creatures that live in them. As I listen to the song, the words become familiar to me, until I'm able to distinguish them clearly. I understand that it's a language I used to speak, and which I now recognize as if it were an old friend I'm meeting again after a long time . . .

He comes and goes from here to there between thick scrub

The god moves his feet nimbly

The nymphs accompany him, walking on the poison of dark waters

The woman stops singing and looks at me. Her lips don't move, but I hear her command clearly:

Come to me

Then I undress and walk toward the inside of the fountain, where her arms welcome me to submerge me in deeper waters . . .

The diary was on the dining-room table, open to the page containing the latest entry. The pen to one side, its cap off, as if Maya had just finished writing, but she wasn't in the house. Arturo usually respected his wife's privacy, yet he knew that when somebody leaves a diary in plain sight it's because they want it to be read. So he sat down on the chair and started from the beginning. He turned the pages with growing unease until he finished. Then he sat musing. He realized he had been worried about Nerea for weeks, when the one in danger was Maya. How could he have been so blind? He only hoped it wasn't too late . . .

His wife's voice broke his train of thought.

'Want some?'

Maya was holding one glass of wine for herself and offering a second one to him. He hadn't heard her come in. Arturo accepted the wine and took a sip.

'We need to talk,' he said.

Maya remained standing. She brought the cup close to her nose and inhaled deeply. She seemed more interested in smelling the wine than drinking it.

'I know where to find Nerea,' she replied.

Arturo set his glass on the table and stood up.

'Don't even think about it,' he warned. 'She's surrounded by dangerous people.'

'You've been looking for her too. Why do you think it's risky for me and not you?'

'Are you jealous?'

Maya let out a burst of sincere laughter.

'No: I understand her better than you.'

Arturo pointed to the diary.

'This isn't a game. The image of Pan has pursued you since you were a little girl. All those men you've seen masturbating in real life and in your dreams, they're a clear reference. And the dream-women you mention, they're the nymphs who always accompany him. Nerea is a nymph's name, so is Maya . . .'

'The nymphs, who are capable of curing as well as causing

madness. You don't have to explain anything to me. I studied the same things as you, remember?'

'I'm scared. I've heard you talking in your sleep. One time you said, "My shadow and I are one." '

'Pan's noontide – ' Maya paused to dip her tongue in the wine. 'The moment when the sun is at its zenith and one's shadow disappears. A moment of transition . . .'

'Is this your way of telling me you're leaving me?'

'Why do you think all of this has to do with you?'

'Why do you want to see Nerea then?'

'Why do *you* want to see her?'

Arturo shook his head. He realized the absurdity of the situation: they were speaking in questions that had no answers.

'I don't know,' he answered honestly. 'I thought I could save her, but now I think she's beyond all help . . .'

Maya approached Arturo. She ran a hand gently through his beard.

'Sooner or later,' she said, 'our true nature separates us from the person we love. Losing one's shadow shouldn't be a tragedy but a goal. It's the only way of finding out who we really are.'

She turned around and started to head towards the bedroom.

'I only ask one thing,' Arturo said with resignation. 'Don't disappear like Nerea did.'

Maya stopped and looked at him with tenderness, as if he were a child.

'You'll see us again. Both of us.'

I no longer need paper to capture my thoughts. The words travel through the air, trace lines on the water. I can have a body if I need one, although for now I choose my immaterial form. I've returned to the source, to the spring from which all stories flow. Finally reunited with my peers . . . The world insists on forgetting us; people hardly remember us, not suspecting the influence we have over them. Even

I had forgotten who I was, but no longer . . . I am your shadow when
your body has no shadow, I am your dreams when you think you have
not dreamed, I am the one who keeps your desire burning even though
you can never have me . . .

A year went by without Arturo receiving any news of Maya.
During that time he became fond of taking long strolls
through the city parks. He fulfilled his teaching duties at the
university, but he spent more time in gardens than in classrooms. He even joined a group of volunteers who devoted
their time to reforesting public spaces. His own house became
filled with plants he cared for zealously. Arturo knew why he
was doing it. He had reread many books of ancient folklore;
the author who supplied the key was James Hillman: 'When
we become fond of certain trees, spots, or landscapes, or try
to hear messages in the whispering wind or consult oracles in
search of solace, then the nymph is doing her work.' Mondragón was still missing; however, no further ritual murders
had occurred. Maybe the Great God Pan had failed in the
forest, but if he sought shelter in the city now, he could rest
easy. There were more and more greenhouses, more and
more citizens were transforming their rooftops into green
spaces. The Green Party had a good chance of winning several mayoral races in the next election. Arturo didn't know
if that would be enough, so he focused on doing all the work
that was within his reach.

Significantly, he avoided one place. He had gone to the
furthest and most secluded gardens in the city, but he turned
his back on the Parque Metropolitano. It was like visiting
an ex's house: you didn't go there unless invited. And that
invitation came in an abrupt manner, while he was watching
the news on TV. The sawmill had received permission to
cut down a significant number of hectares of forest that had
previously been protected. The decision was controversial
and had been made in a backroom deal with the government.

What particularly caught his attention was that not one environmental group appeared on camera protesting. That made him fear the worst.

That night Arturo visited the Parque Metropolitano. He knew exactly where to look. He walked through the section of old fountains until he located a sculpture. Faun for the Romans, Pan for the Greeks. He looked inside. The moonlight lit up the water. On the surface he saw two faces he recognized.

Don't turn around . . .

The voices reached his ear softly, carried on the wind.

'I need to know . . .'

Shhh . . .

Arturo fell silent. The faces of his ex-wives rippled in the water, like in a hallucination. Their hair was down, their faces not made up. They looked younger, the same age.

Don't be afraid. We're all right. Everything is going to be all right . . .

Above Nerea and Maya another figure appeared. It had a face covered in hair and the empty gaze of the dead. Arturo was on the verge of turning around, but a drop fell on the water, distorting the image. When the surface cleared, there was no one's reflection there.

The water was red. More drops fell, painting the fountain crimson.

He looked up. On the shepherd's staff the sculpture of Faun was holding, there was a head embedded. Arturo stepped back, seized with panic. Although it was now covered in stubble, he could recognize the face of Mondragón. His eyes white and stony, fixed on the moment of an awful revelation.

An icy wind blew, dragging leaves and voices.

. . . the war has only just begun . . .

. . . the mind is our territory . . .

. . . we will drive the enemy mad . . .

Arturo covered his ears, but it was no use. A flash of lightning lit the sky. Mondragón's head shook, animated by invisible threads. His lips moved slowly, awakening from a deep sleep, and then his mouth opened in a silent scream.

. . . *it is terrible to fall into the hands of the living god* . . .

Arturo ran between the fountains, through the maze of passageways and gardens. He desperately sought an exit that would take him far from that place, from that city, not realizing that with every stride all he did was enter further into the endless night.

Tlatelolco Confidential

*H*is brain switched on like a TV set. It was night, it was cold and raining, but those details were irrelevant in his new state. He could just as well have been in the desert, beneath a blazing 100-degree sun. Shadows and shapes moved around him. Little by little his eyes adjusted until they were able to focus and discern outlines. Actually he didn't see like a normal person; if he had any notion of the life he had just left behind, he would think that things had the look of a black-and-white photo. However there was one color he could see and which stood out intensely: red. What's more he could smell it. It evoked something in him which he would have formerly described as dying of hunger. And in the place where he was, there was a carpet of blood. He tried to move, but his brainwaves weren't connected with his stiffened muscles yet. The blood caught his attention, so did the movement. Of things coming and going in his field of vision, but also his own. Which he couldn't control yet. Because he was an eighteen-year-old newborn. So strong and at the same time so clumsy. He didn't realize that, of course. There were no thoughts in his head; only an energy, as dark and ancient as the first night on Earth. An energy made of ice and wind. The same which was now reanimating his body, overcoming a torpor which was supposed to be eternal. Just before his joints managed to coordinate with each other, allowing him to rise like an automaton of flesh and guts, something happened. An image from the deepest parts of his former consciousness appeared in his head, making his dead heart beat. From that moment on, it would be superimposed on everything his eyes beheld, providing him a goal besides that of feeding. That image tattooed on his mind was a face. One he could give no name to, nor speak to, nor even recognize. Yet *now all his impulses were drawn towards that powerful magnet.*

Under cover of night and the pre-colonial ruins, the automaton slipped down a side street and left the spot of the massacre.


```
Attn: General Marcelino García Barragán
Secretary of National Defense
Report classification: TOP SECRET
```

It was about 11 p.m., and the situation in Plaza de las Tres Culturas seemed to be under control; however, intermittent gunfire was heard near the Chihuahua Building. As you were informed previously, a number of people were still being held hostage – among them several members of the international press – on one side of the Church of Santiago Tlatelolco, waiting for the right moment for a rescue operation. They were kept against the wall, their hands behind their heads, to keep them from seeing what was happening around them. Near the archeological ruins lay the corpses of thirteen students which hadn't yet been taken away by the cleaning crews. They were guarded by a group of soldiers commanded by Jesús Bautista González of the Fourth Infantry Battalion. Then the inexplicable thing happened. In Bautista's words, everything occurred 'like a slow-motion movie'. Before the soldiers' unbelieving eyes, the apparently dead students began to get up, 'bleeding from their mouths and baring their teeth with the obvious intention of attacking us'. The army personnel responded by riddling the attackers with bullets, without however preventing one soldier from being bitten on the arm. He was treated on the scene and continued with his duties, since the wound was trivial. After the incident, Bautista took precautions: he personally took charge of re-killing the aggressors with a shot to the head. 'They stank

like they'd been dead for hours,' he explained.
'But that couldn't be. I felt we were exhausted
and confused, so I took out a pack of cigarettes
and we all started smoking.'

A few minutes later, when the cleaning crew
finally showed up to move the bodies to the
medical examiner's office, another anomaly was
observed. 'I counted the bodies on the stretch-
ers, and there were twelve,' Bautista stated.
(It should be noted that his statement was taken
on the premises of the Central Military Hospital, where he was treated for post-traumatic
shock. He suffered from violent tremors, his
skin was pale, and he stared into space with
dilated pupils.) Then he added: 'I swear on
my mother that before the attack there were
thirteen corpses. And if one of them was able to
get back up and escape, that can only mean one
thing: there's a goddamn walking corpse loose
in the city.'

Julia didn't sleep. The scenes of the past few hours thronged
in her head like a nightmare. Being in the safety of her bed
only worsened her state of mind. She wanted to go out and
look for Germán, but her parents wouldn't let her. They told
her it wasn't a good idea for her to get involved. That she
should stay home and not attract attention. She would hear
something about her boyfriend soon . . . Julia kept her eyelids
tightly shut, but the tears kept flowing. How the hell had it
happened? That day marked their six-month anniversary;
they decided to celebrate by attending the rally at Plaza de las
Tres Culturas to hand out flyers in support of the students'
movement. And in a single second the world disintegrated in
a hail of bullets. In Julia's mind everything was confused. She
remembered the flares in the sky, the helicopters hovering at
ground level, the shots that started to come from close by.
After that she couldn't reconstruct a sequence of events. She

had isolated images, like scenes out of a horror movie. Only one thing was clear: when the chaos broke out, Germán took her hand and yelled, 'Don't let go,' but in the jostling of the crowd fleeing in terror they wound up separated. Julia was alone among thousands of people shouting or falling with their heads blown off by the projectiles. At the moment when she let go of Germán, she felt as though someone had torn off her arm, although she was unhurt. It had been an internal pain, a tear in her heart. Then she stopped in the middle of the square and started screaming his name. It was like being inside a dream: no matter how much she raised her voice, she couldn't even hear herself. Julia would have stood there screaming until a soldier's bayonet tore her in two, but some friends dragged her towards the avenue, where they got into a passing car. A Volkswagen, Julia remembered that perfectly. What she didn't know was how they had all managed to fit in such a small vehicle. Days later, when she spoke with her classmates, she would learn that many students were helped by drivers who felt sympathy for them as they fled the massacre . . .

Now, wrapped in the twilight of her bedroom, even the silence seemed menacing. The raindrops crawled down the window as though they had a life of their own. And the bundle of her clothes thrown on the floor looked like a crouching animal waiting for the moment to leap on its prey.

Julia clenched her fists and dug her nails into her palms, trying to make that pain drown out the one she felt inside her.

A red brick building. The automaton was incapable of thought, he only followed impulses. His feet had moved until they brought him here. He didn't realize it, but his appearance didn't attract attention in any special way because at that moment a lot of students were walking through the streets in bloody clothes. The image tattooed on his mind generated a pulse, a vibration that connected him to his old self. And it was right in front of the red brick building that he felt it most power-fully. The problem — which of course he didn't perceive — was that he had stopped in the middle of the street. A car approached and stopped beside him. The driver lowered the window and asked, 'Are you all right? Want me to take you somewhere?' Drawn to the sound of the voice, the automaton turned his head. The man at the wheel let out a scream and drove off at full speed. On the corner, a group of homeless people watched the scene. They had improvised a shelter beneath the entryway of an abandoned shop. They had a couple of rickety chairs, a supermarket cart with their belongings. They were drinking 96-proof liquor and sniffing glue. One of them approached the automaton, grabbed his arm, and pulled him towards the shelter. He offered him the bottle and with a toothless smile said, 'Come. You're one of us.'

Attn: Luis Echeverría Álvarez
Secretary of the Interior
Report classification: TOP SECRET

As per your request, various specialists were consulted to shed light on the incident which occurred in Plaza de las Tres Culturas. Doctors, scientists, and psychiatrists agreed that a situation like the one reported by the soldiers is impossible, and that their testimony is the product of mass hysteria, due to the stressful and violent circumstances to which they were subjected for hours.

However — and in accordance with your order not to overlook any detail — I call your attention to the statement of Francisco González Rul, archeologist at the National Institute of Anthropology and History, who until 1964 was in charge of the excavations at the Mexico-Tlatelolco ceremonial site, a post from which he was removed under pressure from developers who were planning to install a reflecting pool surrounding the church and convent of Santiago.

González Rul fell into a deep depression after
his dismissal and was subsequently admitted to
a private clinic, where he remains to this day.

Below is reproduced an excerpt from his
statement:

'I knew that something awful was going to
happen in that place. Bones talk, and I saw the
signals in them. Especially in the so-called
Grave 14. I have dozens of journals with notes
on the subject. The bones had marks, indica-
tions that the fleshiest parts of the muscles had been torn off. Proof of the Aztecs'
ritual cannibalism. Holding a femur in my
hands, I looked towards the square and saw
a wave of blood crashing against the buildings. Tlatelolco was the final stronghold of
the Aztecs during the Spanish conquest, and
it makes perfect sense for their return to
begin from this epicenter. Every tomb excavated, every fragment of pyramid that comes
to light, only confirms that they never left,
that they have only been waiting for the right
moment to take back what's theirs. And for that
an enormous sacrifice was needed. The government thinks it crushed the students' protest,
but the only thing it achieved was to mark the
beginning of the end.'

The following day, Julia avoided her parents' watchful eyes,
slipped out of the house, and with the help of her friend Ana
set out to look for Germán. They visited local government
offices, hospitals, and amphitheaters. The most shocking was
the Red Cross morgue. There Julia saw numerous corpses
brought from Tlatelolco. Mostly students, but also mothers
and children. She noticed that all the corpses were barefoot.
Then a forgotten image from the night before came back to
her mind with the force of a revelation. As her friends were

leading her to safety, she looked down at the ground and saw a strange and hard-hitting proof of the horror: Tlatelolco was a garden blooming with the shoes of the dead . . .

In the evening Julia and Ana ended their wanderings, exhausted and disheartened. Germán was nowhere to be found. And rather than feeling hope, they interpreted that fact as a terrible sign.

When they got back home in the shared taxi, Julia noticed the lights on inside the houses. People were eating dinner or watching television. How could they, after what had happened? For her nothing would ever be the same again. She realized then that there was something worse: life carrying on as normal. Despite what she felt, she wouldn't change places with any of those people moving like ghosts behind the windows.

Memo from the Secretary of National Defense to the Secretary of Health
Classification: URGENT/TOP SECRET

The soldier who was attacked during the incident at Plaza de las Tres Culturas, and who answers to the name of Ernesto Morales Soto, was admitted to the Central Military Hospital owing to a dramatic deterioration in his condition overnight. There is no clear reason for this situation, given that – according to his colleagues' statements – he was only bitten by one of the students. Morales Soto shows all the symptoms of an acute infectious disease, therefore a request has been made for specialists to be sent to the hospital. The doctor treating him suspects a previously unknown virus and fears an outbreak. So far isolating the patient has not been possible, since the hospital facilities are overwhelmed by the large number of wounded admitted in the past several hours.

```
Your prompt response to this emergency is
requested.


Bulletin from the Mexico City Police Criminal
Division
Attention all agents:

The student who participated in the incident at
Plaza de las Tres Culturas and who escaped from
the soldiers' custody has been identified. He
answers to the name of Germán Solís Enríquez
and is considered extremely dangerous. He must
be captured, dead or alive.
  A photograph is attached.
```

It was break time. The students at Vocational 1 were in the main courtyard. The automaton was oblivious to this, but he felt a considerable increase in the energy emanating from the red brick building. He left the shelter, where the homeless people were fast asleep, and made his way towards the origin of the pulsation. The guard at the entrance froze at the sight of him coming through the gate; when he recovered, he grabbed his radio and called the police. The automaton entered the courtyard, causing a stampede of students, who ran and screamed, dropping their soft drinks and potato chip bags. Some remained on the sides, and at the second-floor railing a mass of curious faces peeked out, wanting to snoop from a safer spot. Only one person remained in the center of the courtyard, unfazed as the automaton made his way closer with clumsy steps. Along the way, his right arm detached with a cracking noise and fell to the ground, evoking a new wave of screams.

The image tattooed on the automaton's mind matched the face that was now in front of him.

Julia wiped her tears and gave her best smile.

'I've been looking for you,' she said in a tone of mixed fear and excitement.

The automaton tilted his head. The vibration was at its peak and produced an effect in him that might be called sedative. Julia saw the bullet hole in his chest and lovingly ran her fingers over the wound. She didn't know it, but it was the shot that had taken his life, only ten minutes after their hands separated in the chaos of Tlatelolco. The other hole in him was beside his left eyebrow, it was Bautista's kill shot; the soldier's trembling hand sent the bullet's trajectory through his head without touching the brain.

'Your favorite shirt is ruined,' was all Julia could manage to say at that moment. 'Remember when we went to buy it in Zona Rosa?'

The automaton's eyes twinkled for a moment, then they were a gray gelatin again. A sharpshooter appeared on the roof. Julia could see him leaning on the ledge and aiming his rifle. Her friends yelled at her to get out of the way. The head of the vocational school, barricaded in his office, told her to over the loudspeaker as well. She heard those pleas in the distance, as though she weren't yet fully awake and the noises were seeping slowly into her dream.

Julia made a decision. One which, though she didn't suspect it, was on behalf of all the students who survived the massacre: if life was going to be a nightmare, then she didn't want to wake up.

She brought her lips to Germán's and kissed him.

The sharpshooter got the order. His aim was true: the shot passed cleanly through the heads of both.

Seconds before that happened, and before his living death was snuffed out for good, the automaton responded to Julia's impulse. He didn't kiss her, because he no longer remembered what that was.

What he did was bite her lips.

*

His brain switched on like a TV set.

The soldier Ernesto Morales Soto had just been declared dead. The attending physician covered him with a sheet and turned around, exhausted. Therefore he couldn't see what happened next. His final thought was that he had never experienced a day like that one, and that he probably never would again.

He wasn't wrong.

The automaton pushed the sheet aside and sat up. He had a hunger that the living were incapable of understanding, because it never stopped. It was primal, and its sole objective was to grow until it filled an empty body.

When there are no thoughts, no feelings, no memories, that is all that's left.

HUNGER.

The automaton opened his jaws, leapt at the doctor, and with one bite he unleashed the epidemic.

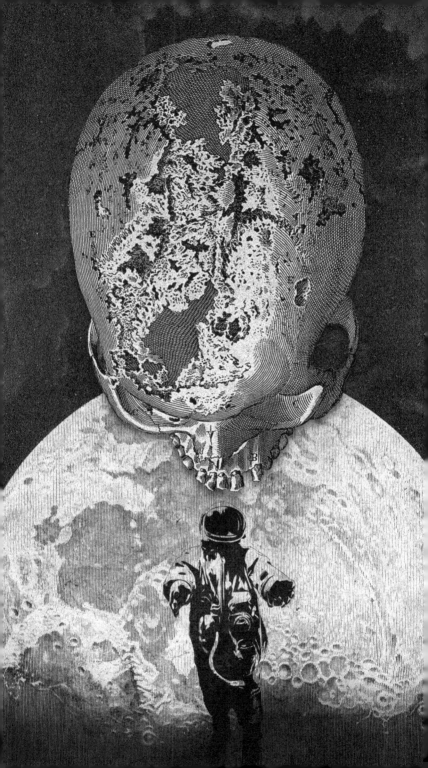

Sea of Tranquility, Ocean of Storms

For Carlos and Jorge, and Jorge and Luis:
in Amado Nervo's house, when
the Moon was still a possible dream.

I n my family there were always secrets, but madness cannot be hidden. During my childhood and teenage years, I watched my cousin Rodolfo's erratic behavior without realizing that what afflicted him was a hereditary disease. To me he was just an eccentric relative who, to top it off, had a twin brother. Rodolfo and Ernesto were fifteen years older than me, but I spent quite a bit of time with them at the family dinners we had at my grandmother's house the last Sunday of every month. My cousins my own age would play soccer in the yard or flip through Spider-Man comics, but I preferred spending time with those twins, who put me in contact with mysterious things. They had a telescope, which they would bring to grandma's house, and when it got dark they would carry it up to the roof and take turns looking at different things. Rodolfo was obsessed with the Moon, while Ernesto's focus was the windows of the neighboring buildings. One of them talked to me about craters and the names of lunar features; the other, about women and what they might be doing behind those rippling curtains.

Everyone has an obsession. Just as I saw my cousins devoted to theirs, I would soon discover mine: telling the stories of other people's lives. From a very young age I realized that my destiny lay in biographies. Reconstructing both the great deeds and the small details that made a celebrity interesting. What I didn't know then was that you have to be careful with obsessions because you can end up possessed by them. I'm not referring to my cousins. Ernesto made good use of his: he grew into a womanizer to be envied. Rodolfo never had a choice: his genes condemned him to detach from reality. The one who started to get into trouble was me, when I stopped editing obituaries and focused on the stories of the living. I became nosy, a voyeur of the events of other people's lives, and for a while some magazines and publishers paid me very well for writing biographies of the famous. But I threw it all away. 'Always better to stick with the dead than the living,' my grandmother used to say.

I didn't listen to her, and what's more, I betrayed my own blood.

One Sunday Rodolfo missed the family dinner. We little ones were told that he'd been in a car accident, that he was in bad shape. Months later he reappeared with crutches. When he finished his rehab he walked funny, like one leg was shorter than the other. Strangely enough, that helped you to tell him apart from his brother, since they were true identical twins.

Like many twins, Rodolfo and Ernesto liked playing jokes on friends and relatives, mixing up their identities. When we younger cousins got old enough to swap comics for *Playboy*s, a rumor started going around among us: that Ernesto couldn't keep up with his conquests, so sometimes Rodolfo helped him out, passing himself off as his brother when Ernesto had made two dates at the same time.

'If that's true,' said José, the cleverest of all my cousins, 'then that can only mean one thing: that Rodolfo is able to hide his limp.'

After the accident, Rodolfo's abnormal behavior increased to the point where the fragility of his sanity was clear. But as the family took pains to hide the dark secret, we had no choice but to seek our own, terrible interpretations:

'Rodolfo wasn't in an accident: his father threw him down the stairs because he couldn't stand having such a weird son . . .'

'He smashed his own legs with a hammer so he didn't have to look exactly like his brother anymore . . .'

'One of Ernesto's girlfriends ran him over when she found out they had tricked her . . .'

The truth, which was revealed to me some time later by my uncle Sergio during a Christmas drinking binge, was starker and crazier. Tormented by the voices that he heard more and more often, Rodolfo threw himself off a pedestrian bridge in an attempt to commit suicide. He survived, but with permanent damage to his legs. What my cousins and I also didn't know was that he underwent numerous surgeries, until multiple pins and implants allowed him to walk again. By the time my uncle lifted the veil on that story, my cousin was confined to his house, cared for by a full-time nurse, and we all knew the name of his illness: schizophrenia.

For a while – when I was starting to earn a living doing biographies – I visited my cousin at his house. He lived in a double prison: the room where he was confined, and his mind, completely given over to intricate, insane fantasies. Carrying on a conversation with him was an exhausting task. Sometimes, without meaning to, he would treat me to images of a strange and sinister poetry.

'Something bad is going to happen,' he told me one afternoon while we were playing chess.

'Yeah?' I replied, thinking about how I was going to get out of check.

After a long pause, during which the tick-tock of the wall clock could be clearly heard, Rodolfo went on:

'I'm absolutely sure that something awful is going to happen.'

I moved my knight to protect my king.

'Why do you think so?'
Rodolfo answered with another question:
'Didn't you hear the silence last night?'

Most of the time, Rodolfo's mind wandered towards convoluted and paranoid plots, in which he always had a starring role. One of his favorites was the one where he got phone calls from a Chinese informant, who gave him confidential information about plans for an imminent invasion of the United States. But it wasn't just any attack: the Chinese had developed a war strategy that involved creating parasitic ramen noodles which – when ingested in soup – would settle in victims' brains and take over their minds. And if you considered how many thousands of cases of ramen soup China was constantly exporting to the U.S., victory was assured.

'And why did they pick you as the one to tell about it?' I ventured to ask him one time.

His answer surprised me. I didn't know whether he regained his lucidity for a few moments and was speaking ironically about his condition or if it was just another of the many manifestations of his fevered ego.

'Wouldn't *you* like to know?'

Nothing had prepared me for what came next. It was something that left me uneasy, and I suppose that spoke well of me, since as a famous psychiatrist I interviewed while writing his biography told me: 'Don't ever get used to crazy people's craziness, because that'll mean you're crazy too.'

I remember Rodolfo was sitting in his rocking chair and looking out the window at the garden.

'This morning I got a message from Neil Armstrong,' he said, as he ran his hand across his chin in a guarded manner.

It was a fantasy I was hearing for the first time, and I was intrigued. The telescope, the dinners at grandmother's house, and other childhood memories came to my mind.

'You mean he called you from his house?'

My cousin laughed condescendingly, like I was a kid who had ingenuously said something funny.

'No,' he said. 'Neil Armstrong is still on the Moon. He never came home.'

In the days that followed, Rodolfo fleshed out the oddest story I ever heard from him. He claimed that the famous astronaut was communicating with him telepathically, and that because of this he was finding out 'the truth behind the events of that strange summer of 1969'. His version outdid the famous conspiracy theory – firmly ingrained in popular culture – which maintained that man had never set foot on the Moon, that it was all staged by NASA with the help of director Stanley Kubrick.

'Yes, they went to the Moon,' my cousin claimed. 'But what nobody knows, and which has been kept secret all this time, is that after taking the first step and saying his famous words, Neil Armstrong entered the surface of the Moon and disappeared. They never found him.'

In my cousin's version, Apollo 11 returned without its most important astronaut, and from the first moment when the crew appeared in front of the media to discuss their feat, Armstrong was replaced by a double.

'NASA didn't want to look bad in front of the whole world if something went wrong,' Rodolfo said, 'so they had arranged a double of each astronaut beforehand.'

According to my cousin, all of this explained many of the things that still weren't clear about the Apollo 11 mission: Why was there no photo of Neil Armstrong on the Moon's surface? Why did Buzz Aldrin, the second man to set foot on the satellite, become an alcoholic after his return? Why did the supposed Neil Armstrong live as a recluse in his Ohio farmhouse and avoid interviews at all costs? And, above all, why, on the few occasions when he appeared in public, was

Armstrong unable to answer one essential question: *How does it feel to have been on the Moon?*

Those suspicions existed: I saw it on the Internet, where I found various forums where they were fervidly analyzed. That didn't prove anything, of course, but it was the only time my cousin's ravings had a basis in reality.

'On the next five missions,' said Rodolfo, 'the secret priority was to find Armstrong. Not that they expected to find him alive, but the recovery of his body became an obsession for the leaders at NASA, a kind of revenge for that first debacle. When they gave up, the Apollo program was canceled, and that marked the end of the Space Age.'

What happened to Armstrong, my cousin explained, was experienced by the astronauts on the later missions as well, only by that time they were prepared. All of them heard a majestic, hypnotic music, a sort of siren song drawing them towards the dark side of the Moon. Those who followed in the first astronaut's footsteps survived because they were attached to the lunar module with special cords. From 1969 to the present day, Armstrong remained 'held' on the Moon and used psychic images to communicate with Earth. A kind of communication that only 'hypersensitive' minds could pick up. In short, the most celebrated astronaut in history was doomed because only lunatics could pick up the frequency of his messages.

'Remember,' Rodolfo told me, 'that as it orbits the Earth, the Moon never turns. It always shows the same face, which is why no one has seen its dark side.'

'And what's there?' I asked. 'Did Armstrong tell you?'

'We are the plague,' he replied, in a cryptic tone. '*They* just want to be sure we never leave our planet.'

'Who are *they*?'

My cousin bestowed another of his good-natured laughs on me.

'You would never understand. Because they are what we are not.'

*

Before work started taking up most of my time and I stopped visiting Rodolfo, my cousin told me one last story about astronauts. He talked about Alan Bean, who traveled on Apollo 12 and became the fourth man to walk on the Moon. After he got back, Bean remained involved with NASA for several years, and in 1981 he retired to become a painter. And the only thing he's painted since are scenes related to the Moon landings. An artist obsessed with the satellite, and with what he and his colleagues experienced there. In fact, one of his most famous paintings is entitled *That's How it Felt to Walk on the Moon*. What that painting shows is Bean himself, wearing his astronaut suit on the lunar surface, surrounded by a mist of intense greens, golds, and violets.

'The song of the interstellar sirens,' said Rodolfo. 'Music with color, but the only one who could express it was Bean. That's why it was so bewitching: it was a trail you had to follow, almost like you could touch the notes.'

'It must be terrifying,' I broke in, 'being hundreds of miles from your planet and feeling there's a force wanting to draw you even further away from it . . .'

'You want to know something?' My cousin's tone suddenly turned gloomy. 'Armstrong and I also communicate with Bean, only he isn't able to understand the messages, so what he does is depict the information we send him in his paintings. He thinks it's his imagination at work . . .'

I stopped listening to my cousin. As Bean was still alive, it occurred to me that I could travel to the U.S. and seek him out to write his biography. Of all the astronauts who had set foot on the Moon, he struck me as the most interesting. The publisher I worked for would doubtless be interested and would pay for my move and the stay.

As if he was reading my thoughts, Rodolfo said:

'There's one painting in particular you have to see. It's called *The Moon Seen from a Dream on Earth*.'

'A poetic title,' I replied, just for something to say, as I got up and put on my jacket. Now I had a new goal: to meet the astronaut-painter.

Before saying goodbye, my cousin added:

'That painting holds the key to everything.'

No matter how hard I tried, the trip didn't come off just then. The publisher had other priorities and work kept piling up. I stopped visiting Rodolfo, but, oddly enough, I began spending time with Ernesto. At that time, my womanizing cousin was going out with an actress my age whose career was just starting to take off. A magazine asked me to do a story on her. I accepted because it would be easy and the pay was good. The three of us went out on several occasions for a drink, but when I started interviewing her, it was just me and her. Her name was Patricia. At first I saw our meetings as part of the job, but before long I realized I was obsessed with her. She was thin, with pointy breasts; she seemed comfortable with her own body and, above all, with her smile: Patricia smiled all the time. Maybe she was just practicing for the cameras, but I had never met a woman with so much self-confidence. She admitted to me that since her teenage years she had gone out with older men, as was the case with my cousin, but that recently she had started being interested in men her age. 'They're not as silly, and they have a lot more energy.' She said it while looking into my eyes, a blatant provocation. I didn't think twice and took the plunge. The days that followed were a whirlwind of motels, drinking binges, and arguments. By the time I realized the mistake I'd made, it was too late. Our fling became public thanks to a photo published in a tabloid newspaper. Ernesto was devastated – or so Patricia told me – and the magazine didn't hire me again because one of their rules was that business and pleasure shouldn't be mixed.

Weeks later, Ernesto called my cell phone. When the phone rang and I saw his name on the screen, I thought about my cowardice, how I should have gotten in touch with him to apologize. It would be the first time we'd spoken since the scandal and I had no choice but to face him. I answered, expecting an avalanche of insults. But all Ernesto said was:

'You have to come. Rodolfo committed suicide.'

I didn't dare go to the funeral and spent the whole afternoon thinking about my dead cousin. I remembered one dinner at our grandmother's house in particular, when Rodolfo used his telescope to show me the unevenness of the Moon's surface. With great patience he showed me each feature and highlighted its characteristics for me. He told me that for Giovanni Battista Riccioli, who had made a map of the Moon in 1651, those shadows looked like seas, and thus he gave them their odd names: Sea of Tranquility, Ocean of Storms, Lake of Dreams, Bay of Rainbows . . .

'The Sea of Tranquility is where all the Apollo missions landed,' he explained. 'It's a perfect spot because it's wide and flat . . .'

And then he added something that I connected with his strange personality, but which now I fully understand:

'That's why you always have to look for the Sea of Tranquility and avoid drowning in the Ocean of Storms.'

That afternoon I cried bitterly because I'd lost one of my most beloved cousins forever. What I didn't suspect then was that one last meeting still awaited me.

Three years after Rodolfo's death, I was in Tucson, standing at the door of an art gallery and space memorabilia shop called Novaspace, which was holding an exhibition of Alan Bean's work. I was in Arizona to interview a snake catcher – a gig for the tabloid that published the photo of me and Patricia – but I was hopeful the gallery would put me in touch with the astronaut-painter. I thought that if I could do his biography, the large publishers would start being interested in my work again. I got to the place very early, after a night of insomnia in anticipation of my visit, and its doors weren't open yet. From its appearance and paint colors, what Novaspace really looked like was a Kentucky Fried Chicken restaurant. If there's one thing the gringos are good at, I thought, it's making everything look boring and corporate. Even a gallery exhibiting the paintings of a man who had walked on the Moon.

When I was finally able to enter, my body resented the blast of air conditioning and I got chills. As I walked past Alan Bean's paintings, my temples pounded and I felt a tightness in my chest. They weren't depressing paintings: they were colorful and depicted the astronauts doing various jobs on the lunar surface. There were only two paintings that expressed feelings. Both had as their protagonist a single astronaut in the same position: arms outstretched and head raised. One was called *Is Anyone Out There?* and the other *Hello, Universe*. Then I realized that my anxiety came from something that the paintings involuntarily reflected: an absolute and suffocating loneliness. Not the loneliness of the lunar landscape, but of Earth's. And I was sure of one thing: if you made the mental and emotional effort to put yourself in the point of view of the astronauts looking at our planet from the satellite, you could catch a hint of the panic of the interstellar abyss. There were no answers up there, and that was palpable in Alan Bean's paintings.

However, one of the paintings did hold an answer for me. When I stood in front of it, it took me a while to discover it. It was the painting my cousin referred to the last time I saw him. *The Moon Seen from a Dream on Earth* showed a lunar eclipse. There was nothing else in it, and my first impression was that it was the least attractive of them all. When I focused on the details, my heart beat faster. The key was in the lower right-hand corner. There I found Alan Bean's signature and a date.

The image had been painted only a month earlier.

*

I fled the gallery in search of fresh air. My head was spinning, my eyes had a glazed look. I collapsed on a bench, breathing with difficulty. I felt an urge to vomit but managed to stifle it. Just then someone came up to me. It was a familiar figure. I rubbed my eyes because I thought I was dreaming. Had my cousin Ernesto really followed me all the way there? Was it a coincidence, or had he found out about the painting from his brother? Maybe he had waited patiently for my trip so he could confirm Rodolfo's triumph in person? Then I realized I was wrong. As always, the revelation came to me late, plunging me into the Ocean of Storms.

My vision cleared. The approaching figure stopped feigning and condemned me with his limp.

Manuscript Found in an Empty Apartment

To: Samuel Luján, Private Detective

Herewith I am enclosing the document requested from this Ministry, in the hope that it will prove of use to you. It should be noted that it is a copy of the original, just as it was found.

Sincerely,

Raúl Solís
Agent, Missing Persons Division
Ministry of Public Safety

I. THE DOCUMENT

My brother Pablo was run over and killed two weeks ago. A taxi crashed into him as he was crossing the street, just in front of the local post office where he was going to mail a package. The news shocked me, even though I was estranged from him and hadn't seen him in three years. He was my only close relative. We didn't have any other siblings and our parents had passed away some time ago. There's no concrete reason why we drifted apart, the only thing I can think of is that his was the world of words and mine that of money. Pablo gave poetry workshops (he had published some poetry collections, *plaquettes* he called them, though it was all the same to me: I never read a single line of his); I'm a stockbroker at a national bank. Now that I think about it, another contributing factor to the distance between us was the fact that Pablo had a knack for picking up women, something that's always been hard for me. While I spent years trying to convince the woman who went on to become my wife – and later my ex-wife – he went from one relationship to another with a satisfied smile on his lips. After my divorce I didn't want anything to do with women for a while, nor with my brother and his many conquests. I never envied him for being a writer. Who in their right mind would choose a profession that hardly anybody cares about, and which yields a measly income besides? The problem was his magnetic ability to attract women despite his precarious financial situation. And not just that: I happen to know that more than one of them wound up paying his rent. The few times we got together for a meal, he spent the whole time talking about the power of words and a theory that sounded to me like something out of a fantasy story: he said that poetry can open gateways to other dimensions. *Real* poetry, because – he explained – there were poets who camouflaged stories in verse. 'Nowadays poets dream of being storytellers,' he rambled on, only interrupting his spiel to ask the waiter for another bottle of South African wine which he would drink at my expense. I would pay attention for a while, but soon my mind would start to wander towards the land of numbers, adding up what we had ordered and what it was going to cost me. Then I'd signal to the waiter for our check, a gesture that marked the end of our forced get-togethers.

After they identified the body, the police gave me a package, the same one my brother was getting ready to mail when the taxi ran him over. It was a manila envelope containing a bulky object. An address in the city of Guanajuato was written on the back, but no name. I threw the package on the passenger seat of my car and didn't open it until later, when I got back home after work. Inside was a book. I don't remember the author, but it was poetry. On the first page there was something written in my brother's handwriting:

> *Amaranta:*
> *I can't do it.*

That strange message touched me, as if its incomprehensible conciseness summed up the story of our difficult relationship. I never did anything for my brother besides treat him to expensive wine in fancy restaurants, but at that moment I knew I had a mission: to make sure that parcel got to its destination. And to meet Amaranta: perhaps she could tell me something about the brother I refused to get close to. I asked for time off work and a week later flew to Guanajuato. I didn't intend to stay any longer than I had to; my plan was to deliver the package and then hop a flight to Acapulco. But my destiny lay elsewhere.

At the Guanajuato airport I got in a taxi and headed downtown. First I wanted to find something to eat and walk around a little. It had been a long time since I'd been to that city, and as I passed through the tunnels underneath it I remembered that it was mysterious by nature; that despite its touristy side, it gave the impression of holding a secret. That impression was reaffirmed when I stepped out of the taxi and started to meander through the mazelike alleys. After I'd eaten, while I wandered through narrow passageways smelling of urine and filled with cigarette butts and broken beer bottles, I remembered my brother telling me once that he was often invited to Guanajuato to give poetry workshops. I decided it was time to deliver the package. I took another taxi, and the address on the back of the envelope led me to an apartment building in a residential area on the outskirts of the city. There was a FOR

RENT sign hanging from the second-floor balcony. I went to the buzzer and pressed 17. No one answered, and for the next ten minutes I got the same result. I decided to wait in the taxi. An hour later, nobody had gone in or out of the building, the meter was still running, and I was out of patience. I thought about leaving the parcel with the superintendent, but I was set on meeting this woman, who rather intrigued me by that time (she had to be pretty, my brother was very careful of his reputation); so I came up with a plan. I pressed the button for the super and pretended to be interested in the apartment for rent. A few minutes later I was led to the second floor by a squat, swarthy man. I asked him the usual questions as we toured the room – how much is the rent? what requirements did they have? were other people interested in it? – and finally I remarked, with all the naturalness I could muster:

'I found out about it from my friend Amaranta, who lives in number 17.'

The superintendent looked at me like I was speaking a foreign language and said:

'You must be confused. Nobody's lived in that apartment for a long time. But it's not for rent, don't ask me why; that's up to Don Eulalio, the landlord.'

I made up some excuse, told him I'd think it over, and left with Don Eulalio's contact information. I decided now not to go to Acapulco and asked the cab driver to take me to a nearby hotel. I didn't think my brother had made a mistake about the address on the envelope. I had no doubt that this woman was his lover, that the book contained a coded message, and I was determined to figure it out. 'Is that how he seduced women,' I remember thinking, 'with poetry and vague messages?'

The next day I spoke to Don Eulalio at his real estate office, telling him I lived in Mexico City but that I would be moving to Guanajuato for work. As he was handing me a photocopied list of the papers and documents he needed, I told him:

'I like the second-floor apartment, but I'd prefer something higher up. The super told me number 17 was vacant.'

Don Eulalio gave me a stern look, the kind you give kids when they say something stupid, and told me:

'Impossible. Somebody's renting it, even though they're not living there.'

'Could you tell me who they are? Maybe I could work something out with them . . .'

The landlord began to grow impatient.

'Forget it. Discretion is an important part of this business. All I can tell you is they're using it for something . . . storage, I think.'

I shook his hand, telling him I would make a decision soon about the apartment for rent and left the office, determined not to leave Guanajuato until I'd gotten inside apartment 17.

Getting inside was easy. The hard part was understanding what I found there. I went back to the building the following day and asked the super to show me the second-floor apartment again, 'to make up my mind'. After he had opened the door for me, some cash persuaded him to leave me alone there. I needed to 'feel the space, as if I were already living there'. The super took the money – in this country even Pandora's box is opened by cash – and told me he'd be back in twenty minutes. As soon as he walked away, I left the apartment and climbed to the fifth floor, where apartment 17 was. Instinct – although in hindsight I can say that it was more a kind of *call* – made me put my hand on the knob and turn it. The door opened without further ado and I went in, though I know now that you shouldn't trust things that open easily, especially when it comes to doors. The apartment was empty. The only thing in it was a built-in wooden bookcase on one wall of the room. It was oval-shaped and full of books. After making sure there was nobody in the other rooms, I inspected its contents. It housed only volumes of poetry. The weirdest thing was that on the first page of every book was written the same sentence:

> *Amaranta:*
> *A key for the door,*
> *an eye for the one-eyed.*

They weren't in the same person's handwriting. In each book the phrase was signed by whoever had written it, and below that was the date and the place from which it had been sent to apartment 17. The dates were all from the past two years and the places spanned the entire country, from Tijuana to San Luis Potosí to Chiapas. Some people recurred, among them my brother. That place wasn't as empty as I'd been told. Someone, at least, had been there to receive and arrange the books. And that someone had to be Amaranta.

I went out of the apartment and left the building, to the surprise of the super. I didn't care; now I had another objective: the post office. I went to the downtown branch and spoke to the manager. I handed over some more cash and told him that all I wanted to know was who received the packages addressed to apartment 17. He summoned a boy with a shaved head who was in charge of the deliveries in that part of town and left me alone with him.

'It's always a woman who opens the door,' he said apathetically, eating a sandwich.

'Is her name Amaranta?'

'Who knows.' He shrugged to reinforce his response.

'One last thing: does she only have one eye?'

The young man stopped chewing and gave me a suspicious look.

'Nah . . . that lady has really pretty eyes.'

The manager called him from the other side of the premises and pointed to the packages he had waiting. I understood it more as a signal to me: it was time to take my ridiculous questions elsewhere.

When I left the place, a man in a black jacket approached me and took out his identification to show me: Samuel Luján, private detective.

'We need to talk,' he said as he lit a cigarette. 'Seems to me like we're both looking for the same woman.'

We went to a nearby café. He told me he had been hired by Amaranta's husband, a rich entrepreneur in the footwear industry, who was suspicious of his wife's evasive behavior. On the very day he started following her, she disappeared. The last place he saw her was in the building with apartment 17.

'She went in and never came out.' He paused for effect and took a long sip of his coffee. 'At least not out the front door . . .'

'How long ago was that?'

'Three months.'

Samuel lit a fresh cigarette. Then he looked me in the eyes.

'And what the fuck part do you play in all this?'

His friendly tone was gone. I decided to tell him every-thing, from Pablo's death to the lonely bookcase in apartment 17.

'That confirms my theory,' said Samuel. 'The bitch went out the back door.'

He took a folder out of his briefcase and threw a handful of photographs on the table. In each of them appeared a woman about forty years old, with black hair and a pale complexion; two intense green eyes stood out on her face. The kid from the post office was right.

'Amaranta?' I asked, uneasy.

'No, the Virgin Mary.'

'What does she do?'

'Wastes what her husband earns.'

'Besides that?'

'She has a cultural center where they give poetry work-shops, but also talks on the occult, tarot readings, and other bullshit. Or what amounts to the same thing: flushing her husband's money down the drain.'

Samuel picked up the photos and left some money on the table. Our meeting was over.

Back in the hotel, I ordered a drink from room service and went online. I needed to check my work emails and forget about this whole mess for a while. But a message prevented me: it was my brother's landlord informing me he was put-ting his apartment up for rent again and that I had to clear his stuff out of there as soon as possible. Then I sensed it: the answer I'd gone to look for in Guanajuato was waiting for me in Mexico City.

Today I returned to the capital. I stopped by the landlord's office for the keys and came to this apartment on Calle de Álvaro Obregón where Pablo spent the final years of his life. Before I went in, I realized why my brother lived there and how the Roma neighborhood summed up his spirit: it was an old community, inhabited by would-be bohemians striving to transform the neighborhood's decadence into something chic and fashionable. Finding his place empty didn't surprise me. Nor did the fact that there was nothing but a wooden bookcase built into the wall, oval in shape, filled with the same volumes of poetry as in apartment 17. What did catch my attention was that there was a single book missing, the last one on the bottom row. And it's not there because it's the one in my bag, the same one Pablo wasn't able to mail. Now I'm writing all this down in a notebook because I know what I have to do and I need to leave behind proof. I don't know what consequences it will bring, but it's the only way of learning what happened to my brother and finding Amaranta.

I'm going to set down the pen and put the book back in its place.

II. THE PHOTOGRAPH

Samuel Luján
Private Detective
Confidential report

This is the last report I'll be writing you, sir. I thought I had found your wife, but I failed. I swear I saw her leave the apartment building where she vanished three months ago. I was staking the place out when she appeared in the doorway. I took several photos of her from my car as she walked down the sidewalk, then I followed her. I waited until she turned the corner, then quickened my pace. When I went around the corner, she was gone. There was a street market and a number of people shopping, but not a trace of your wife. I roamed the area for an hour, searching in every nook and cranny, but found nothing. I thought I was going mad, that my mind was playing tricks on me. Then I went to my office and began developing the roll of film in the darkroom. If she had really come out of the building, as I was certain she had, she would show up on the paper once the chemicals brought her to the surface . . .

One of the people I interviewed during my investigation was a stockbroker from Mexico City who was also looking for Señora Amaranta and who is now missing. I checked up on him to corroborate the story he'd told me and it turned out to be true: his brother knew your wife; he had been run over a week earlier. What he didn't mention was how much he resembled his brother, who was a year older than him: almost identical, the same bald spot and the same goatee framed on a dark-complexioned face. My theory is that the poor sap planned to sleep with your wife, taking advantage of his resemblance to his brother.

I am attaching the document I obtained from a contact at

the Ministry of Public Safety. This file has been responsible for my recent sleepless nights and my growing mental confusion. I have no clear explanation for the contents of these pages; I am turning them over to you so that you can draw your own conclusions.

Along with this report you will also find one of the photos I developed, as well as my resignation letter. I am not the right person to continue with this case. My head isn't working right, and I need to take a break. Of course I won't ask you for my outstanding fees.

In the attached photo, as you will see for yourself, your wife does not appear.

It's a one-eyed woman.

Printed in the USA
CPSIA information can be obtained
at www.ICGtesting.com
LVHW041512171023
761365LV00004B/737